CATACLYSM

Scott Conditt

To my wife and family -
the ones who ground me in truth while I chase fiction.
And to the unnamed, undocumented, unaudited architects
of silence -
your secrets built this story.

THE ARBITER

PART ONE

1

Oh, the things I have seen…

The serene and familiar hum of the elevator as it descends along the cables, plunging three hundred feet subterranean beneath the Pentagon, five days a week for the last twenty years, almost always leaves me in a meditative daze. It's one of the few fixtures within this place that has not undergone dramatic cosmetic changes over the decades. This hub is the unofficial black site, known as Memory Lane, a superhighway of public perception that is under perpetual demolition and reconstruction, with an unknown quantity of miles extending throughout Crystal City. This elevator ride is my Zen space, my quiet place, where I center myself before a shift… even if it only takes precisely one minute and five seconds to make it all the way down to my floor. I've timed it. And it's just the right amount of quiet time to reflect on the greatest hits.

You get to live many lifetimes in this job, replaying the moments, the sights, the sounds, and the angles of it all… at will. I like to imagine myself as some sort of omnipresent, time-traveling god, sitting in my dark cosmic chamber, slipping time, ingesting the top-secret horrors and classified bits of other people's lives, arbitrarily starting them, pausing them, fast-forwarding and rewinding, and even cycling them frame by often tragic frame, all at the push of a button and turn of a dial.

Of the most memorable reels in the archives was indisputably Kennedy's assassination - from the three dedicated camera angles. That's a no-brainer, pun intended. The "Director's Cut" is a multinational masterclass in clandestine cinema and a fan favorite here among the staff, for obvious reasons. Quality-wise, we all know the Zapruder film was akin to bad student filmmaking, which isn't far from the truth of the matter. The other angles, though, the planned ones, those are the crown jewels here. There's a reason they show this monumental undertaking and bit of Agency history to the newly recruited as part of their induction schooling. It's an impressive and foreboding slice of time and a gentle reminder that no one is untouchable. No one. "Loose lips sink ships."

Castro's cameraman framed the action with particularly artful composition and held a surprisingly steady hand, especially knowing the stream of amphetamines those Dominican goons had a penchant for imbibing. Sure, they could take a few notes on proper exposure, obtaining tack-sharp focus, and following leading action - but overall, high marks for selecting such a creative angle. The Russians, however, provided a highly clinical wide frame, not wanting to miss a bit of the action, no doubt, and clearly used a fluid-head tripod to steadily follow the motorcade. The methodical, clinical nature of every nuance behind their shot... from how they dialed the camera's settings for the 16mm film with perfect specs to the unique bokeh and slightly surreal quality that their Soviet-era "nuclear" glass provided ... oh, I could write a dissertation on the mutually brutish and beautiful approach of their methodology.

Our alphabet-soup boys, though, took the award for cinematography and scored the "money shot" on that production, no contest. Which makes sense, as they were hosting the effort, had direct access to the motorcade, and all other nations were merely guests at that particular conspiracy party, each gathering footage as a failsafe and bit of blackmail fodder should the other complicit nations decide to point fingers. B-52s aren't always the deliverers of "mutually assured destruction," after all. Each party had its ammunition in the form of celluloid footage after the operation was said and done. The redundant angles also served as undeniable backups to the backups to ensure the mission was accomplished and not a bait-and-switch. The Agency men had embedded the micro cameras literally within the best seats in the house, with one wide angle embedded in the rearview mirror up front by Agent Greer, who was driving, and one in Connally's seat back. I'll never forget that angle in particular, framing Jackie's beautiful, wide-arching smile under that pillbox hat, watching as her grin suddenly turned twisted and macabre in a flash. The Commander-in-Chief suddenly reeling, clutching his throat... and a mere moment later, his head blossoming and unfolding as the lens was spattered with a drippy, viscous red. Jackie, clambering from her seat, scrambling in her shock to pick up the pieces, as the era of Camelot faded out through the crimson filter and the film reel ran out... What terrible poetry in motion.

That reel took the cake for quite a while. It's one thing to watch modern-day kings and queens come undone, which I imagine is akin to witnessing Caesar's assassination on the Senate steps during the Ides of March. But to be completely honest, I've always had an affinity for the less-than-terrestrial archive footage. This footage is so extraordinary that it still has the Arbiters wagering around the water cooler about its authenticity as an archival artifact versus being some sort of internal plant or sanity check from the higher-ups to keep us on our toes. My keen eyes and level of exposure lead me to believe that we have been fortunate enough to catalog the real deal. With matters of time and space, I think we have seen some real shit.

In particular, the infamously dubbed "Foo Fighters" have always fascinated me, captured by the 415th Night Fighter Squadron tail gunners in November 1944 over the Rhine Valley in Germany. Gritty 8mm film cameras rolled from their sky-high vantage point within the encapsulated bubble canopy of the gunner cockpits. There was something rudimentary yet beautiful and undeniable about the footage. Hoaxes were much harder to fake back then, before every teenager had access to advanced VFX libraries and video editors as throwaway novelty apps on their cellphones. This piece of historical footage is one of my personal favorites for its extraterrestrial implications.

Then, of course, you can connect the dots to the summer of '45 when we unleashed the power of the sun here on Earth during the Trinity atomic test, and again over Hiroshima and Nagasaki later that year. Someone, or something, out there definitely saw the light we created as a beacon across the darkness, signaling that the timeline and growth curve for the Earth apes had accelerated and entered a new era in our evolutionary cycle. Following that, there is the footage gathered in

Roswell in '47. The timing was certainly no coincidence. A conspiracy theorist's squishy dream, without a doubt. Our department trickled and spun up all that delicious data with disinformation to muddy the waters and keep the fog thick for the public, and we have been doing so ever since. By analysis and consensus, it was deemed to be for their own good.

From what little I've seen of the R&D footage produced by the teams in the development sector, the next-generation directed energy technology derived from the tidbits left behind by our otherworldly visitors makes the Fat Man and Little Boy look like cheap Roman candles by comparison. Given these technological leaps, it's no surprise that our elusive little friends have been stealing the spotlight lately, even garnering significant attention in mainstream media over the past few decades. We have managed to repurpose some of their leftovers and recover a few toys, it seems, even if it took over half a century and many casualties in the labs to unlock their secrets. The widespread availability of commercial video technology and cellphone cameras has sped up our official disclosure program. When our collaborators at the *New York Times* "broke" the story in 2020, the plastic pawns on network screens regurgitated the narrative, gushing and guffawing over the playback loop of the globular, monochrome, infrared "Tic-Tac" UFO footage captured by F/A-18 Super Hornets launched from the nuclear aircraft carrier USS *Nimitz* in 2004, or the orbs observed in the Middle East. They were simply seeing and disclosing what we wanted them to reveal - a drop in the slipstream of reality, creating ripples across the surface of national consciousness and slowly normalizing the language, imagery, and concepts of life beyond the stars... all to soften the blow to prepare for a much more eventful day to come.

About fifteen years prior, I reviewed the high-definition, full-color, multi-spectrum footage and volumes of sensor data collected in crystal-clear detail from the scrambled aircraft just hours after the squadron landed back on the flight deck, not to mention the oceanic video and sonar feeds from our nuclear submarines. That was where the real action was happening - deep beneath the ocean. Don't get me started on the Marianas Trench... But what we spoon-fed the public was merely a morsel, a single scrap of Operation Hardboiled. Orson Welles expertly demonstrated what happens when you give the full Monty to the masses all at once - it's overwhelming. Since that little bit of mind theater, we knew it had to be a slow, steady infusion of intel, and that was exactly what our department has been doing for over a century. We control the ebb and flow of information to align with the Grand Plan. It will all come out eventually... all of it. But we control when, where, and how it is revealed, for as long as it matters to the Controllers - that's what truly matters. We turn up the heat slowly to boil the eggs and keep the lobsters from jumping out of the churning pot as they cook all the way through.

When it comes to "the others" out there or the kinds of phenomena that threaten to upend multiple facets of a civilized, well-behaved society all at once, derailing all manner of understanding, dispelling basic social and organizational structures like religion, rewriting physics, and shedding blinding light on our true origins - we categorize those as "Class 5s." This designation is reserved for heavy pills that are detrimental to the business of social order, unless administered with a surgical level of strategy, plain and simple. Oh, and for your information, the debrief on the majority of recent sightings: we aren't alone, but it's not quite what, or who, or... when... you think they might be.

It's not all headline sensations, assassinations, and extraterrestrials, though. Sometimes, it's run-of-the-mill terrorism intel on a perpetual and simplistic scale: murder, mayhem, missile strikes, and sophisticated drones that often miss their marks, taking out entire wedding parties in the many third-world conflicts we police. That's a large part of this job. I observe, I deduce potential outcomes, and I report. The multiple reports logged by my colleagues and me form a baseline for judgment calls, ultimately guiding the hands of the true "powers that be" in our society - not the elected officials, but the unelected officials who control them. The Controllers.

As an illustration, several hundred colleagues and I in the Consortium dedicated over a week meticulously examining and cleaning up the 110 camera perspectives recorded at the Pentagon, in addition to the handful of CCTV and security cameras within sight of the most secure and closely watched building on Earth that significant day - September 11, 2001.

Our team in black scrambled and secured every shot from nearby gas stations and retail stores along the flight path. This was a moment when we had to respond to chaos already unfolding and shape the surrounding narrative. By dawn the next day, the public was already being fed a neatly packaged story: Middle Eastern hijackers, radicalized and razor-wielding, had flown planes into the towers and the Pentagon. Osama bin Laden's name was on everyone's lips before most of the debris had even cooled. The nation was in shock. The crude simplicity and devastating efficiency of the attack had dealt a staggering blow to the country's sense of security.

Imagine the revelation that not only did cave-dwelling terrorists fracture our infrastructure, but a sophisticated foreign adversary also helped orchestrate the attack and successfully deployed a tactical missile directly into the Pentagon. That revelation would have pushed the public over the edge. We had to scrub the records and reinforce the narrative - double down on the guerrilla terrorist angle at all costs, rather than admitting tactical vulnerabilities alongside that already painful reality. One more plane's loss was explainable, but slow-motion footage of a BrahMos missile striking the Pentagon represented an unacceptable truth.

Attackers launched a surgical strike, timed strategically to coincide with the chaos of the Twin Towers attacks, while the nation focused on the skies and New York's smoke filled every screen. This timing was no coincidence; it was a deliberate misdirection. While the world watched Flight 175 crash into the South Tower live on television, a low-altitude BrahMos cruise missile - supersonic, sea-skimming, and of Russian-Indian origin - screamed across the Potomac. It penetrated the reinforced outer wall of the Pentagon like a tungsten-tipped scalpel. Fired from a disguised foreign freighter just off the Eastern Seaboard - a converted container ship equipped with vertical launch cells - it had slipped in under the radar, literally and figuratively. They spoofed the vessel's sonar profile to resemble a typical Maersk cargo hauler. By the time NORAD could have taken notice, it was long gone - vanished into international waters, concealed by a web of forged maritime transponders.

The Consortium's rapid response teams were already on standby deep beneath the blast site. Within thirty minutes of impact, blacked-out SUVs arrived at every gas station, hotel, and convenience store within a ten-mile radius. They confiscated tapes and hard drives, removed DVRs from back rooms, and disabled or destroyed all CCTV systems using controlled surges. The Pentagon's own cameras - those that weren't conveniently malfunctioning - were handed over to internal clean-up teams. Frames were clipped, edited, and scrubbed. In the final version, only a blur, a flash, and a hard-nosed narrative remained: "It was a third plane." Never mind that the alleged pilot failed the flight school in Phoenix for piloting a Cessna...he somehow pulled a maneuver that even expert pilots said would require mastery of such a large commercial aircraft.

Physical debris was curated and planted like a museum exhibit - engine parts from a retired 757, scorched fabric seats, and even burned passports. We constructed the wreckage to fit the story and altered photographs. Just another hijacking. Just another layer to the tragedy. Just enough truth to anchor the lie.

We kept the narrative simple: a pair of soft, gargantuan targets in New York City and the most fortified building on the planet - symbols of our national defense and economic superiority - were equally unprepared and unguarded, exposing themselves as our Achilles' heel. We were brought to our knees for the price of a few airline tickets and some crude box cutters. The vast majority of Americans, in their shock and awe, accepted it.

We learned a great deal about the threshold for accepting absurdity from that exercise. Despite it being open source knowledge that the Pentagon has surface-to-air defenses surrounding it and the most sophisticated military monitoring system in place 24/7, the fact that the only camera angle officially released from the Pentagon guard shack shows just a few blurry frames of "the plane" impacting the south wall is still astonishing to me. One camera angle for monitoring that building? That was our story, we stuck to it, and, mostly, the American people grew weary of questioning it.

Sheeple believe what's most comfortable, what they want to believe, and what's easiest to digest. This tendency reliably works in our favor. Seeing the Pentagon, of all buildings, take that hit in high definition from multiple angles would have triggered World War Three. No one profits, let alone survives, from that escalation. The military-industrial complex does not satisfy its shareholders if the scales tip too far.

Thus, here, far below the impact crater, I and most of those with the rank and privilege to contribute to the Consortium of Arbiters advised that limiting exposure would stoke the flames of conspiracy and cloud public judgment while minimizing external factors that could become further incentivized to disrupt. Giving credit to the unsophisticated terrorists opened the door to a decades-long war and opportunity. Admitting we had been hit right in the nose by a legitimate military adversary would not benefit us.

That's what they call us officially: Arbiters. Most of my colleagues and I prefer "Referees" around the water cooler because, ultimately, we make the calls that dictate how the big global game of foosball plays out. "Refs" for short, like my favorite Dennis Leary film. By design, there are hundreds of us specially trained Refs. Like teams of actual referees on a football field, our singular opinions, deductions, and reports aren't exactly the written law and can't singularly determine the outcome of the game. It's the collective deductions and advisement of the Arbiters in the field, so to speak, that moves the needle in any instance. Hence, the "consortium" bit. The top brass don't technically have to follow our advisement, but they tend to and have reliably done so for over a century now. As a result, things have held together surprisingly well. It's no secret that a few very close calls during the Cold War era solidified the importance of our department's work and contributions, which, without them, we decidedly wouldn't be here as a species today. Kennedy's sacrifice for his country was a large part of that effort.

Observe, report, and advise with high degrees of outcome probability accuracy. That is what we do.

The elevator chimes with its familiar ding, and the doors glide open. The labyrinth unfolds, revealing six seemingly endless white hallways extending from a large circular lobby. An ornate chandelier hangs from the ceiling, refracting slivers of light across the floor - the only true decor that isn't merely a matter of industrial necessity. This is the very chandelier that once hung in the Crystal House, an early 20th-century apartment building in The District from which Crystal City derived its namesake. I always refer to the office as the "alabaster abyss" - an endless series of white corridors, closed white doors hiding countless conspiracies within, and an unending supply of artfully manufactured white noise. In all my time toiling away down here, I've only seen certain sectors of the abyss, relative to my assigned division, of course. There's no telling the true depth and extent of the hive.

2

The Sensitive Compartmented Information Facility, or SCIF, is where I hang my hat for my shift. There are hundreds, if not thousands, of these rooms spread throughout the underground hive. Technically speaking, the SCIF is a room within a room within the hive. To enter the first room leading to the actual SCIF, I swipe my ID card, scan my eye, and palm the biometric touchpad. After my scans and swipes, the familiar "thwomp" of electromagnetic locks disengaging is followed by the slick sound of polished metal gliding on metal as the thick reinforced bolts pull aside. The door then disengages and swings inward on its pneumatic hinges. Inside the storage lock, I meet two of the nameless meat puppets on rotation. They are the "Friskers" - the stale, emotionless praetorian guards assigned in pairs to protect the hive and get handsy with us Arbiters before we are granted supreme access and enlightenment. Each pair of these guards is so uncannily similar in demeanor and regulation appearance that I swear they grow them in pairs from the same embryo in a lab right before issuing them their obligatory "high and tight" haircuts. I don't resent them, mind you; they're a necessary failsafe. I actually feel sorry for them. I mean, what a terrible work detail. I know these guys are likely trained to kill treasonous men with only a paperclip and dental floss, but such alleged talents always seem wasted to me in a role that feels like "the TSA on steroids."

Step one in the safety dance is their magic wand, which I've always found to be rather pointless. I mean, why waste the time metal detecting and radiating my junk with the little electromagnetic black paddle if you're just going to go "hands-on" right after and fondle the hardware anyway? Cut to the chase already. Regardless, the guards go through the same protocol every time any of us Refs enter the storage chamber before being granted full access to the SCIF itself. Wand. Then frisk. Then, they watch tirelessly and simultaneously. Always watching. Not suspiciously or ominously, mind you - but mechanically, emotionlessly. Endless layers of redundancy and bureaucracy form the foundation of the Pentagon. We're on the same team, after all, even if it feels like I am being judged a bit every time, even after decades of doing this. It's the "no small talk, no consorting" protocol. I don't talk to them; they don't talk to me. No chit-chat allowed, as a strict order. It's understood. They just watch as I strip off my personal items: my watch, my phone, my wedding ring, everything down to the receipts and foil gum wrappers that might be floating around in my pockets. Once I'm freed of any "extraneous items" that may be on my person, and the frisking and wanding have begun, the meat puppets flank the master access door and remove their respective security keys from the lanyards on their necks and insert them into opposing paneled wall terminals. In spite of all the upgrades to the facility, this little nod to the Cold War era nuclear launch motif is still in play. It always makes me smile. After a synchronized flick of the wrist by my silent cohorts, the little blinky lights on the stainless steel panel in the wall change from red to green, and the heavy blast-proof security door slides open.

The Observation Deck - my SCIF - gleams. Cold, hard stainless steel walls reflect the harsh fluorescent lights, mirroring the ceiling's identical panels. My stainless steel desk, pristine and unforgiving, is softened only by the surprisingly comfortable German-engineered chair. Its polished surface shines, the built-in padding a luxurious contrast to the austere lines; despite its vaguely erotic, museum-piece aesthetic, it is supremely ergonomic. With all that gleaming steel encapsulating the SCIF, and the insulation that lies behind it, the design thoroughly prevents any type of outward transmissions or electromagnetic interference. It is a Faraday cage, impermeable and a complete void when it comes to any radio or satellite-based transmissions. Nothing in, nothing out. Long hours sitting and watching sensitive content demand supreme lounging capability. I can also dim the lights to suit my eyes and help prevent fatigue.

On the desk sits a security-cleared PC, equipped with heavily shielded fiber optics that connect directly from the terminal's enclosed back to the three-foot-thick floors and walls. This provides a direct pipeline to the top. The PC is isolated from any external Wi-Fi or internet access; all the data and resources I need for searches and research are intranet-based. However, the agency's intranet capacity for data flow and storage far exceed that of the publicly accessible web.

As digitization progressed, every recordable medium evolved, and the scale and capability of our communication pipelines and archiving methods expanded accordingly. It was much simpler half a century ago when all records were stored on a ream or a reel. Cloud computing introduced additional complexity. Now, every security camera worldwide digitally streams and backs up footage to the cloud. The agency developed advanced scraping software to create real-time backups of everything it could capture, and we can even alter footage instantaneously if necessary.

All this data is collected, sorted, and stored in the aptly named "Master Server" floor, which spans the equivalent of a hundred football fields. Two-story-tall server racks filled with encrypted hard drives stand behind the world's most advanced firewall, allowing us to hoard every bit of recorded data transmitted globally that we can access.

An array of media playback devices is at my disposal as well, spanning the evolution of the mediums: DVD, CD, BluRay, DV Tape, Beta Cam, 16 and 8mm projector, even microfilm... You name it; if there was a player or viewing device developed for it, we have it. After reclining in the ergo-chair and logging into the computer terminal with my unique access code, the PC desktop appears. A single file folder has been placed on the black screen labeled:

SITE DD1525.

My assignment.

As always, I begin the real work by clearing my mind. Deep breath in through my nostrils for five seconds to center myself, deep breath out through my mouth for five seconds. Smell the roses... blow out the candle. Let everything else go. This work requires absolute concentration and supreme focus. Zen. Discipline. Everything, every sound, every distraction settles. Then, CLICK-CLICK on the subfolder labeled:

CASE_100702_A_DD0209.

The contents inside the master folder reveal a single notepad document labeled:

Brief

Five sub-folders within this folder populate, each respectively labeled:

1_Hunters
   2_Brains
   3_Law
   4_Brass
   5_Combined

Per procedure, I double-click the included notepad document first. This file routinely contains the meat and potatoes of the intel, the "brief" of the events in question. What agency personnel refer to in military parlance as "The BLUF," or Bottom Line Up Front, this document is a summation of what the source content I am about to review consists of, in very rudimentary form. This brief is compiled by the first tier of Junior Arbiters, also affectionately referred to as Juniors. The role of an Arbiter like myself, AKA the "Ref," is to provide detailed analysis, advisement, and outcome potentials based on the content being reviewed. We conclude and relay our findings to the people who make the final calls. Not the presidents, generals, kings, queens, or C-suite executives that you think hold the power to make the calls. No, we relay the info to the people behind those people. The ones with the real power who shall remain nameless.

Regularly, circumstances dictate these determinations must be swift. So, the notepad is prepared by the juniors with the directive of ensuring it's sterile and factual, devoid of any assumptions or speculative notation. It is intended to advise us Arbiters which aspect of the review we should specifically focus our primary attention on to derive the maximum benefit. Then we forward our analysis and advisement up the chain. It is this distillation of information through the multiple levels of filtration within the organization that is designed to remove contaminants as distractions and white noise that makes the entire system as effective as it is. Think of it as a makeshift survival water filter that first passes scummy, muddy, grit-riddled pond water over coarse stones, then small pebbles, followed by sand, and finally refines the water through the purifying element of crushed charcoal. Every layer the water passes over becomes finer, trapping dirt, debris, and grit until the stream of water runs clear. In kind, the result of our data stream on the other end is clean and consumable data, distilled through layers of analysis rapidly over a very short period.

Time... Glancing at my stainless-steel, company-issued wristwatch, I am reminded that time is always of the essence in my function here.

The notepad reads:

#BEGIN

Location: Advanced Research and Development Site DD1525.

Event: Catastrophic Failure of Critical Infrastructure. Research Technology breach. Unprecedented anomalies observed. Possible biological contamination. Military interventions level 4 ineffective. Heavy casualties. External civilian exposure mitigated.

Outbound Comms: Neutralized. Blackout protocol engaged.

Containment: UAV RECON/IR/THERM/MULTI-SPEC - GRID SURVEY: 97.5% - 99.9% active perimeter intact.

Arbiter Advisement Objectives:

Concealment.

Disinformation Campaign Development and Enactment.

Future Mitigation.

Recoupment of All Viable Research Assets.

Probability of Repeat Occurrence Report.

CONTENT PACKETS:

Hunters - (4) Civilian

Brains & Brass - (3) Science/Research - Contract DoD Site 0209_Col_1215_0322

(6) Mil - BlkSect/SFOD-D, - Q Clearance / Col. Dennings

Law - (1) LEO - Springerville, AZ 34.1334° N, 109.2859° W

Consortium Custodians - Retrieval and Recovery log

STOP#

These are the players and the subjects of my review. Each group serves up a collection of camera angles captured during the event, and they have each undergone preliminary review and were swiftly assembled by our front-line team. The process of distillation involves scrubbing out any non-essential footage, such as black video with no sound detected, and then editing the remaining clips into a linear timeline for my deeper analysis and recommendations, removing any non-essential bits. When in doubt, they would leave footage in play, as I and my Arbiter colleagues are keenly trained and forensically tuned to find shreds of the greater story and elements of intrigue within even the most garbled and grainy frames of footage.

Per my brief, it looks like the theater that this event spilled out onto is a small, bum-fuck town known as Springerville, Arizona. A long-forgotten mining town turned ghost town after the exhaustion and collapse of the local copper mines back in the 1980s. The site lies in a valley surrounded on three sides by mountain ranges. Once a Rockwellian and quintessentially quaint American small town with its own picturesque Main Street, it is now a dusty and forgotten half-mile of mostly shuttered shops and abandoned industrial and scrap yards. With only a few hundred aging residential structures surrounding the town's perimeter and a sparse population on record, the civilian casualties would likely be low - at least for this class of event.

Fifteen miles away from the center of town, via the two-lane highway that serves as the only road in and out, is the Top Secret research facility, Contract DoD Site 0209_Col_1215_0322. It is one of our subcontracted venture sites, a collaboration with an advanced research and development outfit that helps us do some of the theoretical heavy lifting: Dynamic Logistics. The heart of the facility is embedded within the honeycombed and deeply insulated tunnels and massive recessed chambers of the copper mine within the granite desert mountain range, as it had been acquired and retrofitted as a Cold War-era long-term survival bunker designed to be the last holdout for prominent politicians and the elite. It makes for the perfect location to house our specialized team of physicists and their assigned quantum development groups and their work, not to mention excellent environmental conditions for housing the server farms of data being produced within. Per the site file, the nerdy masters of the dark arts that operate within the location are the cream of the independent sector crop at engineering cutting-edge directed energy and experimental matter transportation technology. It is a high-tech hole in the ground for them to ply their trades with no distractions, and we have been pumping a seemingly endless supply of black money down there into the abyss to keep them incentivized and supplied with the latest and greatest tech and tools for almost a decade.

With a destitute town of only three hundred souls topside who are more than willing to take the government subsidy and keep quiet when it comes to inquiring about the specific nature of the work being performed in their backyard, it has been one of our most productive sites. With ample housing and amenities on location, making the quarters the most modern and comfortable available in the area for a hundred miles, most of the government employees and security-cleared private sector contractors, maintenance engineers, and administrative staff who work there only venture out occasionally to frequent the town, visiting the hardware and general stores for common household goods, groceries, and such. They tip generously at the local diner and bar, and aside from that, they mostly keep to themselves, which is advised as per the confidentiality directives of their heavy-handed NDAs and employment contracts. To the locals, who are mostly aging out and dying off, so long as it means keeping their hometown on life support and keeping the lights on, all that they care to know about the government facility and the work being performed there is satisfied under the line that it is being used for "data storage" of some sort. Which isn't entirely untrue, as the secrets of the known universe are certainly being peeled back and archived within the location.

Having a bit of background on ground zero, it is time to digest the angles of the "event" and see what the players who bore witness to it experienced. Double-clicking the folder entitled "Hunters," a video player opens on the computer desktop. Pressing the "play" button, the footage rolls, effectively opening a time capsule and cracking open a window into the critical and final intertwined moments of others' lives.

THE HUNTERS

PART TWO

3

A slate of information appears in white text on the computer screen: the rundown and diagnostic data of all the sources that comprise the video footage obtained in the field for this linear timeline of events. It reads:

THE HUNTERS SOURCE CONTENT
- GoPro HERO 12 - 4K/60fps
- AccuShot - Weapons Mounted HD Camera - 4K/60fps
- Canon R5 - 4K/60fps
- Sony A7iii - 4K/23.98fps
- Apple iPhone 13 - 4K/60fps
- Samsung Galaxy Note - 4K/60fps
- Sionyx - Aurora Color Night Vision - 1920x1080/60fps
- DJI Mini 3 Pro - Aerial / Drone / 4K/60fps
- GameTrail Pro - Trail Camera - 1080p / 24fps
- IRIRay MICRO 384 12 Micron 25mm Thermal Imager / 1080p / 24fps

Timecode and location data appears in the upper left corner of the screen, tracking the exact or approximate timeline of when the displayed footage was recorded, as assessed by the Junior Arbiters.

04:13:27 09/02/22 Springerville, AZ - 34.1334° N, 109.2859° W
Sony A7iii - 4K/23.98fps
PLAY.

From the passenger-side window of a vehicle, the inky bluish-purple pre-dawn horizon rolls by. The telltale silhouettes of saguaro and cholla cactus, guardians of the Sonoran Desert, occasionally break up the skyline. The camera turns around, handheld, revealing a man in his early 30s, handsome and rugged with a beard, wearing a camouflage hunting jacket. He yawns and then grins wide into the camera.

"Happy almost first light, ladies and germs. Steve Waller with Field and Hunt reporting from the beautiful high desert of Arizona. It's about 4 a.m., and I'm on the road with my old war buddy and hunting guide extraordinaire, Mikey Langner..."

Steve quickly whips the camera around to film the driver, Mike Langner. Mike, sporting a mustache and wearing a weather-beaten camouflage hunting jacket, remains silent, responding to the prompt for camera time with a single, extended middle finger.

"Oh, come on, man, our poor viewers at home! Now I'm going to have to edit that out. Sorry, folks, he's a man of few words, but we'll forgive him because he's a hell of a shot and a moderately decent hunting guide," Steve quips, prompting Mike to grin back at the camera.

"Decent, huh? I seem to remember being the only one with a filled tag on the last two hunts we went on," Mike replies wryly.

The lens quickly spins back to Steve as he positions it on the vehicle's dash and refocuses on himself, feigning embarrassment. "Alright, alright, you're sort of a big deal. So, today, we are on the outskirts of Springerville, Arizona, headed to pick up Connor, a student of Mike's whom he's been training for his very first hunt. We're going to a ranch outside of town that has a feral pig problem, and we're going to see if we can't help bring home the bacon. That about right, Mike?"

The camera turns back to Mike as he chimes in, "Yep. Easy first hunt to break in some gear and shake off the nerves. A little nuisance animal hunt that also helps out the local ranchers."

"And because it's private land and we're targeting pigs that are considered a nuisance species, we can even get some nighttime shots in and use the new night vision units and thermal optics we're bringing along. You can't use those on traditional seasonal hunts. With a first-time hunter who's middle-aged, this is a new angle for the video series we're calling 'Late To The Game.' We hope it inspires all of you out there who may be new to the hunting lifestyle later in life and encourages you to get out there and get after it," Steve says in his best presenter voice.

The camera cuts. Static.

05:00:14 09/02/22
Sony A7iii - 4K/23.98fps

Filmed handheld from the cab of the truck, the outline of a single-story ranch-style house comes into view as the headlights wash over it. It's dark outside and the porch lights and a single window are the only spots of bright illumination against the pre-dawn sky. The truck rolls to a stop; Mike gets out and walks to the front door. Before he can knock, a slender forty-year-old man dressed head-to-toe in crisp, modern Kryptek camo gear, with a hunting pack slung over his shoulder, appears, grinning widely as he reaches out to shake Mike's hand.

"Connor, good to see ya, buddy. You weren't kidding. This place is really out here. Hey, looking sharp - nice gear," Mike says. The man, Connor, looks pleased with the approval and slowly turns to show off his new camouflage hunting gear, resembling a child showing off his Sunday best before church service.

"Yeah, I thought it looked cool. Ordered it online. The pattern's pretty neat. Hope I got the right stuff," Connor replies, pivoting his attention to the camera, which is now closing in. "Oh, hey man. This must be the camera guy, your writer friend, Steve, right?" Connor awkwardly waves to the camera and extends his hand as Steve reaches out from behind the camera to shake.

"Hey, buddy, yeah, nice to meet ya. Thanks for agreeing to let us document this experience. I'm looking forward to sharing your story," Steve says warmly from behind the lens.

"For sure. So, I'm just curious, is this going to be on YouTube, or - " Connor begins, but Mike, clearly growing impatient, interrupts.

"Well, shall we get going? First light breaks in about forty minutes, and then I figure we have a couple of hours to set up base camp, scout the area a bit, and see what's already moving out there. If we hurry, with any luck, we might get a few shots off before it gets warm and they bed down for the afternoon. Then we can head back out for nighttime opportunities," Mike says purposefully, clearly eager to adhere to the schedule and get on the move.

"For sure. Let's get going. Town's only about thirty minutes away. It's a bit of a drive, but when it comes to work, I like to be just close enough to be far enough away from it all, ya know?" Connor says as he moves toward the truck.

Mike stops, holds up a hand, and looks at him, raising an eyebrow. "You sure you aren't forgetting something?"

A long pause follows as Connor considers this question. Mike mimes leveling a rifle against his shoulder, aiming and discharging. Connor immediately realizes his error. The camera shakes as Steve chuckles from behind it.

"Shit. My rifle. One sec," Connor says, quickly ducking back into the house.

Mike turns to the camera. "First-time jitters..." he says, shaking his head as he walks toward the truck.

The camera follows, and Steve quips, "I mean, he's your protégé. I just thought you'd have taught him better, is all."

Mike climbs into the truck and starts it up. "He's an engineer, what can I say? All brains, zero field experience. We're gonna fix that, though."

The two experienced hunters chuckle inside the truck as the camera focuses through the windshield on Connor, now with his rifle bag slung over his shoulder, locking the front door to the house and jogging to the truck. "Sorry, fellas. Now let's do this!"

The camera cuts.

4

05:25:42 09/02/22
  Sony A7iii - 4K/23.98fps
  GoPro HERO 12 - 4K/60fps

The sun has painted the sky with purples and fringes of light blue on the horizon. Mike is driving the truck, with Connor sitting alone on the bench seat behind the driver, next to a stuffed hunting pack and some supplies. Through the rear window, we see a side-by-side all-terrain vehicle is being towed on a trailer behind the truck. The angle from the passenger seat looking back alternates between the handheld camera in Steve's hand and a GoPro mounted on the dash, capturing all three men in a dedicated fisheye wide shot as they drive.

"Alright, Connor, I'm gonna be rolling for most of the trip, so get used to it, buddy. Now let's get your personal backstory while we're driving, and save some memory card space for the fun stuff on the trail. Give us your story, brother. Who are you, what do you do, and why are we here?"

Connor looks a little nervous but happy to be there. He obliges. "Oh man, okay. Well, I'm Connor Mayhew, forty-two years old. I never hunted growing up. City kid, ya know? I always sort of felt like it was something I had missed out on. So, after I bought my first rifle, I linked up with Mike here through a mutual buddy and started taking basic marksmanship and firearms courses this past year."

"One of my best students. Legit," Mike chimes in.

"Turns out my background with numbers and calculations as an engineer lends itself pretty well to long-distance precision craft," Connor says humbly.

"Nice! What kind of work do you do?" Steve follows up.

"I'm an engineer, working for a defense contractor, one of the big three. But don't get too excited; I don't get to do any of the cool laser-guided stuff for the pointy things that go boom, as we say. I just work on theoretical physics-based algorithms, the numbers that feed into all that cool stuff. My office does some subcontracting for the research center out here. We'll actually see the general area of the mountain soon as we get closer to town. That's why I suggested this spot for feral hogs; I always hear the ranchers in town complain about them tearing up their fields," Connor explains.

"That sounds very cool, and way above my pay grade. I didn't know there was any real industry out here in BFE," Steve says, intrigued.

"Yeah, it's pretty interesting. I've only been out here for a few months on a contract assignment. The company I work for, Dynamic Logistics, helped build out an old decommissioned Cold War-era bunker that had actually been constructed within what used to be an old copper mine back in the 60s. They turned it into a secure data server farm with a pretty substantial research lab. That's where I hang my hat, doing joint research between my work and theirs."

Mike chimes in, keeping his eyes on the road. "Hope they're paying you well. This town is about as dead as it gets; it has been for decades. But being able to do some off-season hunting and clean up hogs on a private stretch of land is a perk."

Connor laughs at the camera. "Yeah, definitely not a place I would want to call home long-term. Not much to do out here, and it's far from just about everything civilized. But the pay is good, and their facility - at least the parts I have access to - has some cool tech I get to work with. I think the money that DL pays out to the town is keeping it on life support for now, to be honest."

"Nice, man. So, back to the hunt. What do you hope to take away from this experience?" Steve asks.

Connor thinks for a moment before answering, "I hope we get a few hogs, but I really just want to apply everything Mike has taught me in a real-world hunting scenario. When the pressure is on and my blood is really pumping, I want to know that I can be confident with my gear and my shooting, especially before deer and elk season. I've done so much work in controlled settings at the shooting range, and I just want to feel like I'm one hundred percent ready." The camera holds on Connor for a moment as he looks thoughtfully out the window. He's sincere and focused on achieving this personal goal.

"Excellent. Well said, and nice job. That was great. Thanks, brother," Steve says.

"Yeah, of course. Thank you. Hey - there's the mountain! That's 'DL,' Dynamic Logistics, where I ply my trade, as they say," Connor says, pointing ahead through the front windshield.

Steve turns his camera, focusing, zooming, and refocusing the lens through the dirty windshield. A mountain range in the distance comes into view against the horizon and the slowly brightening purple shades of daybreak. Two small beacons of light can barely be seen pulsing on the hillside, possibly aircraft warning lights - the only sign of industrial development on the otherwise brown and craggy mountainside, which appears to be a massive dark silhouette, like the edge of a torn piece of paper against the sky.

"Welcome to Springerville, gents," Mike says as the vehicle passes a green road sign stating the same.

The cameras cut, then resume. The timecode shifts.

05:39:17 09/02/22

An old gas station clerk with a ZZ Top-length beard, dressed in greasy coveralls with a name patch that says "Carl", leans against the truck trailer and chats with Mike at the gas pump while Connor fills up the truck. A police cruiser is parked at one of the four nearby pumps. Everything about the gas station and the leathery old clerk, who stands a sentry to the pumps, is weathered and faded, looking like it hasn't changed much since the '80s. The camera pans over the gas station where the hunting party has stopped and focuses down a long stretch of what looks like the town's Main Street, a quiet row of red brick shopfronts and a few stoplights signaling to empty roads. The camera angle then pans slowly in the other direction down the road leading away from town, across an adjacent two-lane highway that seems to stretch on forever into the flat, brown desert terrain. Off-camera, the polite exchange between the gas station clerk and Mike can be overheard.

"Good luck to you boys out there. Them pigs been tearing up the few good fields we got left, rooting through 'em something fierce. Makes it so the cattle be breakin' their legs, getting stuck in all those holes. The old man gazes vacantly out at the desert terrain, shaking his head in disdain. "It really is a damn shame. Filthy swine."

The door chime from the gas station entrance jingles as a fit young police officer exits the station, a water bottle and bag of jerky in hand. He observes the hunters and the old man and notices the camera filming as he exits.

"Be careful out there too. There's still a few of 'dem Mexican timberwolves out there from back when liberal tree-huggin' assholes shipped 'em in," the grizzled old gas station clerk says in a rough drawl.

"Still got wolves out here?" Mike inquires. "I thought they were all driven out."

"Yeah, they released a bunch of those Mexican Grays years back. Some bullshit about wildlife diversity and such. All they did was kill a bunch of cattle and a few horses and get out of hand... Should put 'em all down, ask me, along with those feral-ass pigs. Only good thing about the wolves is they do eat some of them swine from time to time, no doubt. But dem wolves almost killed a few boy scouts camping with their troop out there a few years back, I hear. No good, no good at all," the gas station clerk mutters matter-of-factly before hocking a loogie onto the road in disdain.

The police officer grins as he removes the gas pump from his cruiser and chimes in "You guys heading out to do some hunting, I take it?"

"Yes sir. On public land. Looking for pigs." Steve responds.

"All good, fellas. Be safe and don't you boys let ol' Carl worry you none. We haven't seen a wolf in ten years. Most you gotta watch out for is snakes and scorps. Just be sure you shake your boots out in the morning."

Carl scoffs. "Heya, Dusty. I told you, I hear those damn devils at night howlin," he replies.

The officer, Dusty, rolls his eyes and looks to the camera and with Carls back to him shakes his head and waggles his finger in a circular motion by his head, the hand sign for "crazy".

"Well... we will sure do our best," Mike says, grinning and removing the gas pump nozzle from his truck and hanging it back up.

"Thanks for the heads up fellas."

The camera holds for a moment on the old gas station clerk as he stares off at the sunrise, thumbs tucked into his coveralls. It's likely the most interesting part of his day has now concluded. The camera cuts.

5

07:09:11 09/02/22
  Canon R5 - 4K/60fps

A slow panning shot of a campsite setup plays. Three small tents encircle a fire pit, where a camp stove and an ice chest are set up nearby the side-by-side. Connor emerges from his tent and waves to the camera enthusiastically.

"Home sweet home for the next few days. We're all set up here and will be heading out within the hour to scout for pigs. The ranchers said we could use bait, so we might set out some corn feed, see if we can draw them in if needed," Steve narrates to the viewer. The camera pans across the valley and holds on the mountain range. The two pulsing beacons of light from Dynamic Logistics on the mountainside can barely be seen at this time in the morning. "It is beautiful country."

Camera cuts.

07:35:11 09/02/22
  GoPro HERO 12 - 4K/60fps - 4K/60fps

A POV shot from Connor's perspective appears as the GoPro action camera mounted to his chest rolls footage. Steve can be seen stepping away from the camera, as he must have just activated the recording. Mike steps into the frame holding a bolt-action rifle with a small cylindrical camera fixed to the front of the stock.

"Hey, Steve, I mounted this camera to Connor's scope. It seems secure. Do you want to check it out and make sure it's set up right?" Mike asks.

Steve turns his attention to Mike as he takes the rifle.

"Damn, man, nice rifle. Springfield Waypoint 2020? Carbon fiber barrel? What's it chambered in?" Steve admires the bolt-action rifle.

"Yeah, it's chambered in 6.5 Creedmoor. Mike recommended it. I've got the Leupold glass on there, and I've really been enjoying the setup," Connor says proudly.

"Hell yeah, I bet! That thing's a tack driver." Steve presses a button on the AccuShot weapons-mounted camera. "Okay, so we just power up this scope cam here..." A new angle appears on the screen.

Intercut GoPro HERO 12 - 4K/60fps /AccuShot - Weapons Mounted HD Camera - 4K/60fps

The point of view captures the view through the rifle's scope as Steve takes the firearm and levels it downrange toward the horizon. "Yeah, this should capture your shots and let the viewer see what you see right through your scope. Sound good?"

"Yeah. I don't have to do anything with it, just aim?" Connor asks.

"Yup. Don't even worry about it. The settings allow it to auto-capture footage thirty seconds before and after each time the rifle fires. We'll roll on your GoPro and this camera on your rifle to capture the action from multiple angles. You don't have to do anything. I want to give the audience your perspective and let them see what it looks like to be on the hunt from your point of view. I'll monitor and control everything remotely with the apps. Just stay focused on making your hits - pretend the cameras aren't even here, cool?"

"Yeah, sounds cool, man. No worries," Connor responds.

"Yo, Mike, do you mind if Connor takes a shot? Maybe try it out to make sure we didn't shift his zero when we set it up?" Steve asks.

"Yeah, good call. Connor, you see that white rock a hundred yards out there between those two patches of cholla?" Mike points out the area and target he is spotting for Connor.

"Out there? By the vein of black rock?" Connor asks to confirm.

"Yeah, exactly. Go ahead, toss your ear protection on and chamber a round. Let's see where we're at with it. Take your time - make your hits count," Mike says, adopting the tone of a patient instructor.

Connor strips a 6.5 Creedmoor round from his rifle's sling, which also doubles as an ammunition scabbard, and loads it directly into the chamber of the bolt-action rifle. Mike plugs his ears with his fingers, and Steve puts in two foam earplugs as Connor chambers the round and starts to take aim.

The view through the scope cam displays an illuminated reticle in the center of the scope's crosshairs as it hovers momentarily over the target - the white rock downrange - before settling as Connor composes himself.

"Remember your breathing," Mike calmly reminds his student off camera.

The sight picture steadies on the rock as we hear Connor control his breathing: deep breath in… deep breath out… deep breath in… deep breath out… BANG! White powder puffs as chunks of the rock explode.

"I'd say you're still zeroed," Mike says.

"Alright, you guys about ready to scout?" Steve asks as he fires up another handheld camera.

Canon R5 - 4K/60fps

The frame focuses on Connor, holding his rifle and grinning. He safeties his rifle and pulls his hunting pack onto his back. With the GoPro camera mounted to his chest rig and the newly fixed scope camera on his rifle, he proudly poses like Hemingway, hamming it up a bit for Steve's camera.

"Let's make history," Connor says.

"Nice shot, man! You feeling good? Ready to rock?" Steve asks.

"Good, man, ready to roll. Let's get it," Connor replies cheerily.

Camera cuts.

07:47:12 09/02/22
GoPro HERO 12 - 4K/60fps

The camera is mounted to the front roll bar of the side-by-side as it traverses the rocky terrain. The engine revs loudly as it bounces and climbs along the desert floor.

Camera cuts.

07:59:56 09/02/22
GameTrail Pro - Trail Camera - 1080p / 24fps / IR

An extreme close-up of Steve's face abruptly fills the frame as he fixes a game trail camera to a tree. He pulls away from the camera, revealing the parked side-by-side in the background. The image auto-adjusts its brightness and contrast to the ambient light of the location.

"Alright, we've got a little corn feed laid out here in this sector about a quarter mile away from base camp. With any luck, the pigs will smell it and circle up for a snack. This trail cam should ping my cell via the app, and hopefully, we can get on top of them pretty quickly if they trip the motion sensor. It's got infrared for the nighttime stalks too, letting us see these little bastards in the dark. Ain't technology grand?" Steve comments to the camera before giving a thumbs-up and hiking back to the side-by-side, revving it up to catch up with Connor and Mike.

08:06:11 09/02/22
DJI Mini 3 Pro - Aerial / Drone / 4K/60fps

The distinct buzz of a recreational drone sounds off as the aerial view of the surrounding scrub brush and the endless desert horizon fills the frame. The distinct ridgeline of the mountain range that houses Dynamic Logistics is visible far off in the distance, serving as a geo-reference point. The terrain moves along swiftly as the drone picks up speed, and its gimbal-mounted HD camera tilts down to offer a true bird's-eye view straight down. The desert floor is mostly sandy, barren, and rocky until a few steep cliffs and crevices appear, followed by green belts lining the canyons below. Distinct blue fingers of water appear as they carve through the trenched recesses and form a small but significant stream. The drone continues to fly and circle, its speed slowing down as it reaches a clearing. Below, three figures come into view, all looking up at the remote-controlled craft while shielding their eyes from the morning sun. As the drone hovers and descends, one figure is clearly holding a remote control. Moments later, the drone drops at breakneck speed, stabilizing ten feet above the ground, and its camera focuses, revealing Steve, Connor, and Mike by the side-by-side. Touching down in a quick blast of dust, the propellers whir down almost instantly, and Steve approaches the drone.

"Well, fellas, we've got a stream a quarter mile west of here. What do you think, Mike? You think the pigs will be bedding down by the water?" Steve asks.

"Mmh-hmm. Thick brush, water, mud… I bet a hundred percent that's where they bed down. Good looking out," Mike replies, eyeing the horizon where Steve pointed out the stream. "Let's hit that ridge before we roll down there and glass for a bit. See what might be moving around before we head into the thick of it."

Drone camera cuts.

08:37:31 09/02/22

Mixed Footage: Canon R5 - 4K/60fps / GoPro HERO 12 - 4K/60fps / AccuShot - Weapons Mounted HD Camera - 4K/60fps

Mike is poised on the edge of a ridge overlooking a seventy-five-foot drop into the ravine where the creek bed is located. He has one eye up to a spotting scope as Connor kneels next to him with a pair of high-powered binoculars. They quietly scan the creek below for any sign of movement.

Camera cuts.

08:42:55 09/02/22

Mike points downward. As the camera follows the direction of his finger, we glimpse Connor, excitedly peering into the ravine. Below, through the foliage and brush, the camera focuses on three pigs: two are fat and older-looking, clearly more robust and mature than the smaller pig, which is half their size. Each hog exhibits the distinct characteristics of a feral hog, with elongated snouts and filthy, matted hairs caked in mud. They meander slowly through moderately thick brush near the waterline, occasionally rooting in the earth at their feet, completely unaware of their stalkers above.

Mike turns to the camera and whispers, "Let's pack up and hike down. I don't want to risk a shot through that bush from up here. I think we can get a clean shot from the ground, and we should be able to follow those tracks easily."

Cameras cut.

08:50:01 09/02/22

* * *

Mike leads the trio on foot, stalking quietly down the embankment near the water's edge, pointing out fresh tracks in the mud along the way. Connor attentively mirrors his mentor's movements as they stalk their prey. As they round a bend in the stream, a small outcropping of large boulders offers them some cover. Mike signals the group to stop and slowly points down the path past the boulder outcropping, about forty yards away. The pigs have stopped at a puddle to drink, and a clean shot is now in view.

Connor moves alongside Mike and unslings his rifle. Mike whispers some instructions that can't be heard on camera, and Connor methodically kneels, pulling a loaded magazine from his pocket. In smooth, silent motions, he pulls back the bolt on the rifle, inserts the magazine, and slides the bolt forward, chambering a round. He takes aim, and the camera captures his every movement, with Mike nearby for Connor to steady his breath and settle into his aim.

AccuShot - Weapons Mounted HD Camera - 4K/60fps

Through the rifle scope's POV, the crosshairs waver between the two larger pigs before finally settling on the one closest. The reticle positions itself right behind the pig's shoulder and steadies... BOOM! A round discharges. The pig goes stiff-legged as if struck by lightning, then violently kicks as it falls over. The other two hogs squeal, startled by the shot, and tear off haphazardly, crashing through the thick brush nearby. Their speed is surprising, especially compared to their previous lazy demeanor. They vanish from sight in an instant.

08:37:31 09/02/22
   Mixed Footage: Canon R5 - 4K/60fps / GoPro HERO 12 - 4K/60fps / AccuShot

"Chamber another round. Be ready to clean up," Mike instructs. Connor follows suit, preparing and leveling his rifle for another shot while maintaining focus through the scope, ready to finish the pig in case the first shot didn't do the job. After about ten seconds, Mike relaxes and motions for Connor to lower his rifle. Steve operates the camera, following from behind as Mike and Connor approach the pig, visibly loosening up the closer they get.

"Congrats, buddy! Your first blood. You bagged a swine in one shot."

Clean too!" Mike says, and Connor grins back at the camera.

The camera circles around the two celebrating hunters and pans down to capture footage of the pig. Huge, hairy, and beastly, it lies on its side, tongue hanging loosely from its mouth, with a clean, dark red hole punctured in its side. A pool of crimson slowly oozes from beneath it as subtle tremors twitch through its legs.

Off-camera, Steve interjects, "Tell us what was going through your mind, Connor, and what you're feeling right now."

"Oh man, that was intense. It felt like time slowed down, right? I just kicked into gear, tried to remember to control my breathing like we trained, and getting on target was a rush. I didn't want to miss, you know? It gets a lot more serious when it's not on paper and a real animal is in front of you. I was worried about wounding it. But it worked out. I'm happy it was one and done," Connor says, clearly amped up from the adrenaline of the shot.

"Fantastic placement, right behind the shoulder blade, buddy. He was done before he knew it," Steve comments.

"Alright, this thing's coyote chow now. Let 'em feast. Nice job, Connor. You want to scout for another one?"

"Hell yeah!" Connor exclaims, clearly eager for more hunting.

Camera cuts.

11:37:31 09/02/22
Mixed Footage: Canon R5 - 4K/60fps / GoPro HERO 12 - 4K/60fps

Shaky footage filmed from the backseat of the side-by-side as it cruises through the desert, with Mike and Connor in the front seats scanning the horizon for signs of movement. The GoPro is mounted on the roll bar, filming the vast expanse of desert stretching into the distance, the engine noise drowning out all other sounds.

Camera cuts.

13:45:31 09/02/22
Mixed Footage: Canon R5 - 4K/60fps / GoPro HERO 12 - 4K/60fps

Connor stands before the camera in an interview-style setup, while Mike stands in the background, scanning the skyline with binoculars.

"Alright, go for it," Steve can be heard saying, cueing Connor to speak.

"Well, the day started solid. I bagged a pig in the first few hours after we set out. But now, in the afternoon, we haven't seen a single one. Mike says it's probably because it's hot out. Those two that took off must have bedded down deep in the thick brush of that ravine because we couldn't track them or get a read on them, even with the thermals. But we're still scouting, still looking for any sign of - " Connor quiets as an unusual but distinct howling cuts through the air.

Steve shifts the camera's focus to Mike, who has lowered his binoculars and is smiling as he turns to the camera, nodding his head. "Wolves... that old bastard wasn't kidding. You hear that?" The howling trails off, and moments later, it is matched in intensity from afar, answered by another similar but distinct cry.

"Holy shit, man! That's incredible..." Steve says enthusiastically.

Steve refocuses the camera on Connor, capturing his reaction, which, by the look on his face, is more concerned than elated.

"Do we need to worry about that?" Connor asks earnestly.

"Nah, man, they've got plenty to eat out here. Just be careful when you go to take a piss at night that you don't stray too far from the campfire. Those things will come out of the darkness and bite your dick right off," Mike says, smirking and clearly enjoying teasing Connor.

The howling continues as the camera captures Connor's and Mike's reactions, both listening to it echo across the landscape, each man appreciating the raw nature in his own way.

Camera cuts.

16:47:11 09/02/22
AccuShot - Weapons Mounted HD Camera - 4K/60fps

A mature, weathered hog is lined up in the crosshairs as it roots around in the dirt with its long, bristly snout. Suddenly, the scope camera jolts violently as the rifle discharges. Pink mist jets from the pig's side as it falls dead in its tracks. Connor and Mike can be heard celebrating the well-placed shot just off camera.

"Yes! Well done, man. Two for two," Mike commends his star student.

"Nice. You ready to test your skills with the thermal and night vision?" Steve asks off camera.

"Definitely. Feeling good and comfortable. Looking forward to stretching myself with that now," Connor replies, his confidence swelling after this last kill.

"What do you fellas say we head back to camp, get dinner started, and prep the gear for the evening and nighttime stalk?" Mike suggests.

"Definitely could eat. I'd like to get a few B-roll shots of you two and the landscapes for the video as we make our way back, if that's cool?" Steve adds.

Camera cuts.

17:11:56 09/02/22
Canon R5 - 4K/60fps

A beautiful scenic wide shot captures the sun setting over a rolling field. Scrub brush dances in the wind against the blending colors of the skyline, transitioning seamlessly from yellow to warm orangish-reds on the low horizon and darker bluish purples higher above. The silhouettes of Connor and Mike appear, driving in the side-by-side as it enters the frame from the right. They motor slowly across the desert, the engine a faint hum at this distance.

Then, steadily, the unmistakable deep pulsing bass of rotor blades cutting through the air begins to fill the otherwise serene setting.

"What do we have here...?" Steve can be heard saying off camera, clearly caught off guard.

The camera jiggles and is abruptly pulled off what must be a tripod, quickly panning to the sky just as the outline of a Blackhawk helicopter blurs overhead, traveling low and fast.

"Holy shit!" Steve exclaims as the camera shakes before regaining focus on the chopper. It zooms off toward the southeast horizon, heading straight for the mountain range, becoming shrouded by the mirage of exhaust contrails mingling with the blazing orange of the final sunset. The camera zooms in, attempting to hold focus on it as the helicopter approaches the faint pinpricks of pulsing light on the range, right where Dynamic Logistics is located.

"Huh..." Steve mutters just before the camera cuts.

18:30:56 - 19:22:17 09/02/22

A time-lapse shot of the campsite reveals a fire, with Connor, Steve, and Mike moving in blurred motion. Through the rapid movements, the men prepare a meal over the fire, transitioning pots and kettles, lifting the lid on one pot, and stirring something that emits steam. They then sit down in camp chairs for a brief moment to eat. As they do, the last light of sunset dims rapidly, transitioning from evening to the darkness of night, while stars fill the sky above like shards of glass, catching glimmers of light.

Camera cuts.

21:01:47 09/02/22
GameTrail Pro - Trail Camera - 1080p / 24fps / IR

In infrared, everything resembles a creepy black-and-white X-ray image, with eyes glowing eerily. A fat hog appears on screen, rooting its snout through the corn feed piled generously around the base of the mesquite tree to which the camera is attached. "MOTION DETECTED" flashes on the screen as a motion sensor icon appears in the upper right corner next to the Wi-Fi and Bluetooth icons.

Camera cuts.

Mixed Footage:
    - Sony A7iii - 4K/23.98fps
    - Sionyx - Aurora Digital Color Night Vision - 1920x1080/60fps
    - IRay Thermal Imager / 1080p / 24fps / Thermal

In vibrant contrast to the monochrome infrared image, a multicolored gradient fills the frame. Thermal imaging. The distinct outline of Mike's facial features appears in warm colors, with cooler tones highlighting his ball cap and the edges of his jacket and body.

"Whoa, badass, man! It's like Predator vision. Get to tha' choppa!" Connor exclaims, doing his best Arnold impression.

"Yeah, buddy. This unit is like the scope cam you used earlier; it records similarly but lets you see anything with a heartbeat out there in the darkness," Steve tells Connor proudly.

"Super cool…" Connor says as the camera pans around the terrain, presenting the landscape in the same spectrum of color.

"And we have this little guy… a pretty cool new colorized digital night vision unit by Sionyx. Check this out. We can use these to scout and film what we find as well."

The image shifts from the psychedelic colors and textures of the thermal scope camera to a Technicolor version of black-and-white night vision. With a limited color palette on the clothing and the nearby scrub brush appearing in vibrant green, the landscape resembles midday, albeit with unusual contrasts and shadows.

"Whoa… that is trippy. It kind of feels like cheating with all this gear," Connor comments.

"Well, yeah… I mean, it definitely is. That's why it's illegal to use for actual hunting. But it's great for pigs on private land, nuisance animals, and predators - stuff like that," Mike chimes in.

A cellphone DINGs an alert notification off-camera.

"Oh damn, we've got a live one on one of the trail cams, boys. Perfect timing! Look at the size of this pig!" Steve exclaims, holding up his cell to show the image of the pig recently captured on the trail cam for the others to see. "Let's put this gear to work."

Camera cuts.

6

21:31:26 09/02/22
  Mixed Footage:
  Sony A7iii - 4K/23.98fps
  Sionyx - Aurora Digital Color Night Vision - 1920x1080/60fps
  GoPro HERO 12 - 4K/60fps
  IRay Thermal Imager / 1080p / 24fps / Thermal

Warm orange, red, and yellow blobs of blended color combine to form the image of the hog in the distance as it sniffs and roots at the ground, eating corn from the feed pile.

"Just the one?" Steve asks quietly.

"Yup. Solo," Mike whispers back in his usual calculated and concise manner.

The image switches to the color night vision camera, showing the same scene from a different angle, but more clearly in the technicolor-style night vision display. The hog remains unaware of the hunters as it continues gorging.

The thermal scope's digital crosshair reticle centers on the pig's chest, wavering slightly as the animal moves slowly around the corn feed.

"Take your time, buddy; we've got plenty of it. Make it count," Mike whispers off-camera to Connor.

"Copy that," Connor replies, as the camera's microphone picks up his deep breathing technique, which he has learned to help steady his aim and calm his nerves.

The crosshairs stabilize once more on the pig, just inches behind its head and at the base of its shoulder blade.

The rifle discharges. A spray of warm colors bursts in the thermal viewer from the pig. The animal squeals loudly, its startled death cry echoing across the desert. It runs ten feet before staggering; its front legs bend and go limp, and then it suddenly slumps down onto its face, flopping to the ground in a small cloud of dust.

"Did I get him?!" Connor asks excitedly.

In response, the sky over the mountain range crackles with jagged electric-blue streaks of lightning, most manifesting directly above the two subtle beacons of light on the mountain. The distant beacons of Dynamic Logistics appear to act as a sort of lightning rod, attracting the electric fingers from the heavens. Oddly, there are no clouds in the sky.

Then, in a volley of flashes and rolling thunder, arcing spiderwebs of light ripple from the mountain range, their crackling points touching down across the desert landscape and illuminating the ground below each blast in a rolling shockwave of electric-blue light. Each craggy arc, accompanied by the coinciding crackle and pop, resembles an enormous bug zapper gone haywire.

Suddenly, as if triangulated by some unseen force, the light pulses conjoin, intensifying in energy as they absorb into one another, finally concentrating over the fresh corpse of the downed pig. The beams intensify and center directly overhead, creating a macabre spotlight that blindingly illuminates the ground below. The camera feeds glitch and interlace as the electric bursts interfere with their recording capability, garbling and distorting the imagery captured.

Click. PAUSE.

With the click of a mouse, the playback REWINDS.

Click. PLAY.

The cameras continue to glitch and cycle as the electric bursts ignite from the ether, seeming to dance around and probe the pig carcass.

PAUSE.

Through the glitching video from the color night vision camera, the image is adjusted, and the contrast is sharpened while paused. Amidst the intensity of electric arcs whiting out one half of the screen and the digital distortion garbling the other, an odd shape begins to clarify. Switching to the thermal imaging perspective, traces of the same anomaly appear in the warm hues of thermal imagery. Looming over the downed pig's corpse is the outline of something both unmistakable and unnatural: long legs, appendages that must be arms, and a craned neck attached to a conical, sloping elongated head. The video feed advances frame by frame, and the twisted, blurry form of the anomaly on screen seems to pour itself into the pig, and then, in the next frame... it is gone entirely. The playback freezes on the image, then advances a single frame at a time. The pig retains its warm orange and yellow heat signature at its center as the frames progress, the lightning dissipates, and along with it, the light.

21:39:15 09/02/22
GameTrail Pro - Trail Camera - 1080p / 24fps / IR

The low-fi sound recording of rolling thunder trailing off in the distance complements the IR image on screen. Subtle flashes of lightning flicker, rolling away from the camera and fading far out near the horizon line as they finally subside. Fifteen seconds pass with only the light breeze stirring the branches of a nearby creosote bush ever so slightly. Then... IT appears, even if only for half a second on screen. Large, musclebound, and incredibly fast, the creature darts past the mounted trail camera in a blurred flash. Its body is covered in fur, distorted due to its speed as it runs past on four distinct appendages with large, plodding feet. Whatever it is, it becomes even harder to formally identify due to the dust it kicks up from the desert floor as it moves. The most unnerving aspect of what is captured on screen, however, is the intentional glance it seems to offer directly to the hidden trail camera, which films in secret, using only undetectable infrared illumination. Just briefly, before disappearing from view in a blur, the glint of two points of distinct specular reflection is visible. Unmistakable, undeniable, undeterred... eyes looking back.

THE BRAINS and THE BRASS

PART THREE

7

A slate of information appears in white text on the computer screen, detailing the rundown and diagnostic data for all the sources that comprise the video footage obtained in the field for this linear timeline of events. It reads:

THE BRAINS & THE BRASS SOURCE CONTENT - VIDEO
   - Security Camera Array: Multiple Source Angles, Condensed - 1920x1080/24fps
   - Laboratory Documentation Camera Systems: Multiple Source Angles, Condensed
   - 4K/60FPS- Laboratory Employee BodyCams: Multiple Source Angles, Condensed
   - 4K, 60fps- DL Primate - VISOR POV / HUD - 4K, 120FPS
   - Canon R3, Lab Documentation Camera - 4K/60FPS
   - SPEC OPS Helmet Cams (x4)

Timecode and location data appears in the upper left corner of the screen.

09:03:11 - 09/02/22

Springerville, AZ - 34.042845, -109.231243
Location: DL Advanced Research and Development Site
DD1525.Security Camera
- Temporal Lab, Observation and Control Room

The mounted camera in the corner of the room captures multiple glowing PC screens within curved, built-in, wraparound consoles. The illuminated displays ensconce the softly lit observatory along three of its walls, while the fourth wall consists entirely of steel framework and floor-to-ceiling ballistically reinforced clear polycarbonate. Beyond this bulletproof wall, the view extends into a vast chamber carved into the mountain. At the center of the cavern, a long suspended metallic pipe, at least ten feet in circumference based on the size of technicians in hazmat suits walking nearby, runs the entire length of the space. The massive pipeline disappears around bends at both ends of the cavern. Every four feet or so, massive loops of riveted copper coil around the circumference of the pipe. However, the three scientists in the main control room above seem particularly uninterested in their colleagues beyond the glass below, remaining glued to their glowing computer screens.

Above each of the three lab-coated personnel working diligently at their respective terminals, text denotes their names and titles within the research and development site. "RODERICK DAVIES - LEAD LAB ASSISTANT" appears over the tall, lanky, shaggy-haired thirty-something, who is craned over his terminal, which is littered with empty energy drink cans and candy wrappers. He intently scans data on the screen while his fingers flit across the keyboard with blistering speed. Clad in a black Deftones band t-shirt beneath his lab coat, he jams out to music through earbuds as his feet clad in red Van's sneakers nervously tap and shift on the tile floor beneath him.

Two terminals down, in stark contrast to her neighbor, sits "LI MENG - Deputy Chief Scientist." Her workstation is organized with paper notebooks, Bic pens neatly aligned by color on either side, and a small succulent arrangement. With her hair tied in a tight bun secured with hair sticks, she maintains perfect posture while peering over thin wire-framed glasses at her screen. She types calculated, delicate keystrokes on her keyboard, as if playing a demanding piano piece. Pausing every few lines to examine her inputs, she quickly scrolls through color-coded graphs on her secondary monitor to reference the data points. All the while, she bites her bottom lip, considering her entries before proceeding with her work.

Finally, at the back of the room, holding a tablet and stylus while examining a computer screen, is a well-manicured gentleman in his late fifties, "DR. JOSIAH TURNER, PhD." Refined and poised, with an intense steely gaze fixed between screens, the silver-maned doctor sports a neatly trimmed beard. He appears both perturbed and intrigued by the complex geometrical charts and graph animations fluctuating on his monitor.

Moments pass as the lab coats continue their routines. Then, the heavy steel-reinforced observation deck doors glide open. A stocky redheaded man in his forties, wearing a navy blue blazer and khaki slacks, enters the room with an air of authority. He pauses after entering to examine the chunky gold wristwatch on his wrist. The text on screen identifies him as "CHARLES DARBY, SITE MANAGER." Eyeballing the room down his nose, he claps his hands together to garner attention. Darby addresses the preoccupied occupants.

"Alright, party people, today is the day!"

All eyes in the room reluctantly turn to Darby, their lack of amusement evident; they've seen this routine before. As Darby runs his fingers through his thinning hair, he scans the laboratory. He quickly ramps up his feigned enthusiasm and sidles up to Dr. Turner, making no attempt to disguise his movements as he conspicuously peers over Dr. Turner's shoulder to see what he is working on. Swiftly ending the unwelcome gaze, Dr. Turner casually logs out of his terminal and backs away while side-eyeing Darby with annoyance. The doctor sets down his tablet on the corner of the console and addresses Darby like a pestering child, not concealing his disdain for the interruption.

"Charles, per the manifest, we still have a full shift to prep our procedural demonstration here. We intend to use every minute to cross-check the inputs to enhance the chances for success. What is it exactly that we can do for you right now? Every second counts in ways I can't begin to articulate to you in a fashion you'd have any chance of comprehending."

Darby holds his hands up in feigned surrender, acting shocked.

"Joe, I am offended and hurt, but mostly hurt! Of course, you do. You're precisely correct, as always," he fires back, snide and biting.

"I mean, you and your little team have been milking the clock for the last six months. What's squeezing the last few drops out of the clock going to hurt? Right?!"

Darby laughs to himself while nodding to Meng and Davies, who barely glance at him from across the room, each shaking their heads in disbelief at his oafish approach while trying to stay focused on their work.

"You, my friend, have until precisely..." Darby checks his wristwatch for dramatic effect, "...four o'clock. Then you better have everything dialed and buttoned up, ready for the demo, my friend! The Top Brass expect it to work!"

Darby clearly relishes the authority he holds over his captive audience, punctuated by his sardonic grin.

"Just saying, this better go off without a hitch, or it's your ass, not mine. You understand that, right? This is your last opportunity."

Darby leans uncomfortably close into Dr. Turner's personal space, staring at him dead-eyed like a stalking bird. Although scholarly in appearance, Turner does not flinch at the gross gesture of intimidation, as one might expect. Instead, he casually and calmly removes his spectacles, pockets them, and leans slightly into Darby's invasion with a hint of a grin, as if to imply he is not only ready for physical conflict but is also more capable than one would perceive him to be - and even welcomes the invitation to square off.

Something in Darby's psyche triggers a more restrained nature, and he quickly adjusts his posture and tone, acting as if he were merely joking. He steps back from Dr. Turner and turns away, slowly strolling through the lab.

"Easy, big fella! Ha... got the ol' Doc riled up. I'm just applying pressure; that's my job, you know.

"The fuel cells for your experiment are en route. The Element 115 is confirmed. I came through with what you said you needed; now it's your turn, Joe-Joe.

"Get your little team of minions ready to put on the full fireworks display, because this demo needs to be the one, the big winner, to get the seal of approval for the contract.

"So, do us a favor, okay? Just make sure the damned thing is failproof," Darby says, blotting his sweat-beaded brow with a tissue as he hovers over the back of Meng's chair, making the poor girl cringe.

"In science, there is no such thing as a failed experiment, Darby. We successfully collect data every time we make an attempt," Dr. Turner says, holding his back to Darby.

Darby bristles, white-knuckling the back of Meng's chair.

"The only thing you'll be collecting if this doesn't fly is

unemployment, Turner," Darby fires back. "You know… every other department is hitting their projected targets and development goals this year. But for some reason, we keep funding your half-baked blunders." This noticeably irritates Dr. Turner.

"Well, the other departments aren't exactly deconstructing the foundational elements at the very core of spacetime…" Dr. Turner replies. Darby merely scoffs and rolls his eyes.

"Time is up, Doc. Ten years of R&D will be scrapped, flushed down the drain if this doesn't go as well as you promised. I'll make sure the closest you ever get to working a lab again will be scrubbing shit streaks as a janitor for some po-dunk community college in Bakersfield. Your protégés here will be sanitizing the damn chimp cages down in Biomechatronics for the rest of their contracts if this doesn't go stunningly well today. So, chop-chop! All hands on deck!"

Darby suddenly studies his gold wristwatch again, punctuating his impatience with disdainful sarcasm.

"Speaking of all hands… I'm late for check-ins with the other teams. You know, the producers who are actually keeping the lights on in this dungeon."

Davies and Li remain quiet, but their glare conveys how they feel about Darby as he exits the observation deck and the reinforced doors glide closed behind him.

"God, I pray he gets rectal cancer," Dr. Turner says aloud. Davies and Li chuckle, the tension broken. "Alright, back to it. Davies, review the adjusted input points. Li, let's run another simulation, full render, please." The team resumes their work.

Meanwhile, just down the hallway outside the lab…

09:08:34 - 09/02/22
Security Camera - Hallway A

Charles Darby shuffles down the hallway while tapping away at his cell phone screen. His impatient pecking is interrupted by an incoming call, which he quickly answers.

"Darby here…. Yes, yes, sir. I just interfaced with them, actually, and…. yes, yes, absolutely. We are ready to go here, I assure you. I'd say we're ninety-five percent good to go on this one - "

Darby pauses as he is interrupted. His demeanor grows grim, serious, and borderline defensive.

"Sir, no, I hear you, but tying me to the outcome doesn't seem fair. I am pushing them as hard as I can. .... Of course... Yes. Yes, I understand. I do, yes, I know that."

Darby stutters and quiets, listening to the other end of the line. He visibly deflates as he leans against the wall to listen before cautiously proceeding.

"But if I may, sir - "

He is cut off. Turning red in the face, he wrings his hands and looks nervously up and down the hall to ensure no one is eavesdropping.

"Understood. Okay. Yes. I will report back as soon as the demonstration is complete. I have complete confidence that..."

He cuts short. Darby looks at his phone screen to confirm what he knows to be the case. Confirmed, the caller disconnected. Darby slumps for a moment, then lashes out, punching the air and wringing his hands in frustration as he swallows curses and his own venom. Then, he stills, gathers his composure, adjusts his tie, and continues walking briskly down the hall as if nothing had happened.

Camera cuts to:

09:19:45 - 09/02/22
Security Camera - Biomechatronics Lab, Pod A

The Biomechatronics lab contains three distinctly segmented pods, or zones, within it: A, B, and C, each housed within the massive granite-walled warehouse space resembling a Hollywood movie studio soundstage. In total, the space spans ten thousand square feet or more, with ceilings that must reach at least four stories high, inclusive of catwalks, lighting rigging, and cable runs tethered above. Pod A is the largest zone, occupying much of the open floor space upon entry to the lab. A massive letter "A" is stenciled on the wall of this zone, while Pods B and C are marked by their alpha designations painted on the floor-to-ceiling glass and steel-reinforced observation walls that encapsulate each self-contained space. Their letter assignments are also stenciled in smaller detail on the sliding security doors, which have keycard access terminals embedded in them. These two smaller pods are located at the far end of the warehouse, adjacent to one another.

Dressing the wide-open main stage of Pod A are several simple yet precise fixtures. To one side of the space, a half dozen steel-framed cubes with sides measuring approximately two feet each are positioned haphazardly next to one another, seemingly in no particular order, as if they had been carelessly rolled out onto the floor like large dice. Nearby is a series of climbing apparatuses resembling old-school steel-framed jungle gyms, complete with ladders, monkey bars, and a few simple staircases that appear to lead climbers up one side's forty-five-degree incline and then immediately down the opposite side. There is also a single two-story wall formed of sheet metal, framed in and supported by steel beam scaffolding. Along the face of the wall, several window openings, absent of glass, provide access from one side to the other.

All of these architectural fixtures are painted white and have a slight glossy sheen. Small black circular decals featuring yellow "X" markings across their centers are plastered on every flat surface, step, or handhold throughout the space. These symbols resemble the signature markings placed on the now antiquated crash test dummies featured in old slow-motion industrial testing films. Back in the day such markers' actual purpose was to serve as tracking and placement markers for the half dozen high-speed film cameras used to capture the carnage. The footage allowed engineers to make scientific deductions regarding specific rates of velocity, force outcomes of impacts, and the various effects such trauma would inflict on the expressionless subjects had they been made of flesh and bone, like their creators. Just as it was then, a number of video cameras are stationed on wheeled tripods around the main floor, actively capturing and tracking every movement taking place within the room.

Unlike the inanimate crash test dummies of old, however, the humanoid-shaped representatives demonstrating their skills and abilities before their fleshy lab coat-clad human counterparts are far more animated and adept at avoiding collisions. The squad of polished alloy robots in Pod A are maneuvering, contorting, crawling, climbing, and executing high-precision maneuvers throughout each obstacle or task-based area. The team of engineers and scientists mills about the space, tapping at tablets while chatting with one another as the bots accomplish their tasks. In one corner of the space, three bipedal humanoid-shaped robots lift and stack the heavy steel-framed cubes like dutiful warehouse workers. The bots create tall, neat stacks, scaling higher than their own "heads" in the corners of the testing zone. They move smoothly and calculatingly, their reflective alloy glinting with each pivot as they avoid collisions while swiftly navigating around one another. The commercial assembly line application benefits are obvious, as the bots move in choreographed unison, stacking the blocks perfectly in line with one another.

Like world-class free climbers scaling a mountain face, a team of mechs lifts and pulls themselves through the empty windows of the vertical wall, flowing easily through the next window higher up, and then back down again in an endless figure-eight loop of climbing and descending along the structure. Others go prone, leveling their chassis perpendicular to the floor in a plank-like maneuver, then crawling through a small rectangular air duct-shaped structure before emerging on the other end and traversing a series of stair steps. Only then do the bots pause, seemingly scanning their next route and objective, before deftly maneuvering along a thin overhanging ledge leading to their next obstacle. They're not all completely modeled after the human form, however. In the far corner of the room, a four-legged dog-like robot gallops up to an all-white sedan and uses its craning articulating neck and pincer-like "jaw" to delicately open the vehicle's door handle. Then, just like an eager canine, it climbs in and takes a seat in the rear of the vehicle as if awaiting its owner's next command.

Amidst all of the ongoing demonstrations, Darby can be seen entering the space on the security camera. He motions impatiently to one of the nearby lab technicians, an enthusiastic young man in his early 20s, who quickly rushes to personally deliver a pair of clear safety glasses and earmuff-style hearing protection to Darby. Although the audio is muffled in this segment of the video, Darby looks nonplussed and begrudgingly affixes both to his head, mumbling impatiently before gesturing swiftly to the technician with something like, "just get on with it." Darby folds his arms and leans against the back wall of the room, biting his fingernails while seemingly becoming lost in his own thoughts. Clearly, the officious man is still troubled from the call he took moments before in the hallway with a significant figure of authority over him. You don't have to be a trained Arbiter to draw that conclusion or discern how fragile the obnoxious man's ego, not to mention his position, within this organization seems to be.

In spite of Darby's irritable mood, the young technician eagerly picks up a nearby tablet and taps a few entries into it before giving a thumbs-up across the vast space of the warehouse to yet another one of his fellow lab coats working behind a small glass-walled control room.

The switchboard operator returns the young tech's thumbs-up and then manipulates a few dials on his board. A series of yellow warning strobe lights around Pod A begin flashing all along the walls of the sector.

Then, a section of the floor near the young tech begins to glide aside, pulling back to reveal a chamber beneath the very floor itself. From this crevice, a row of new bots begins to rise.

These mechs are all similar in design to the shiny metallic models performing tasks and maneuvering throughout Pod A's main demonstration zone, aside from their finish and notably skeletonized and more angular portions of their frames. These particular models appear to be more refined, lighter, but also somehow more rugged, with a matte powder coat of dark charcoal grey covering every inch of their frames and all of their connective cables reinforced with thick, corrugated, rubberized tubing.

Each of these dark bots also bears a deep maroon-colored numeric designation, with 01 through 07 stenciled on each of their respective shoulders and torsos.

The young technician swipes his tablet, and the bots all activate, stepping in servo-driven unison up to the red line painted on the floor before them. The recess in the floor that they emerged from smoothly glides shut.

Moments pass before a barrel-chested technician clad in a blue jumpsuit briskly enters the room from two large steel pneumatic doors, struggling to push a roller cart fitted with a heavy rack of automatic rifles, belt-fed machine guns, and several ammunition boxes.

No one behaves alarmed, as everyone in the room simply goes about their own business and continues running their own demonstrations and tests. Just another day at the office.

The technician in the blue jumpsuit struggles to stop the cart's momentum but manages to line it up right next to the standing row of robots, all poised at attention along the thin red line painted on the floor.

The young lab tech initiates a few swipes and presses another command.

Instantly, Robot Number One pivots on its claw-like hydraulic heels and steps up to the weapon rack.

The automaton swiftly and precisely extends its arm and firmly but gracefully grasps an FN 249 SAW machine gun from the rack.

With its articulating double-joint hinged fingers, the mech inspects the firearm, turning over the large armament and opening the chamber as it racks the bolt before flawlessly feeding a belt of ammunition from one of the ammo boxes into the open slot.

The mech surveys the chambered weapon before closing the bolt and holding it at the ready, like a soldier standing at attention and awaiting orders.

The technician chuckles, giddy with the robot's performance, grinning widely like a child steering a remote control car successfully at the park, showing off for all the other kids. Darby, however, looks unimpressed and sighs impatiently while continuing to pick at the skin of his cuticles. The lab tech gets the point and proceeds without needing a formal invitation. Another swipe and press of the technician's finger, and the robot takes a few steps forward, standing directly on a yellow line painted on the floor a few paces in front of the rest of his squad. The technician swipes again, then inputs another command. Thick, clear walls of bulletproof glass glide up from slices in the floor, safely closing off the space containing the bots from the other zones and occupants within Pod A. A long crevice in the floor fifty feet ahead of the armed bot cracks open, and a single white-painted steel target, shaped like a human silhouette mounted to a rod, emerges. Nothing but the far wall of the immense warehouse space lies beyond the target. Swipe, press. The robot shoulders the rifle and aligns its singular slit "eyeball" sensor with the holographic weapon sight mounted atop the armament. A moment later, a deadly and deafening blast erupts from the barrel as a barrage of rounds impacts the steel target precisely in the center of the chest. A brief pause, and the only sound echoing off the high ceiling is the tinkling of brass shell casings on the concrete floor. The robot swiftly pivots its torso without moving its feet, adjusts aim, aligns its sights, and another volley erupts. Twenty rounds impact the upper cranial portion of the steel torso target. The bot's precisely placed impacts never land more than a centimeter or so from one another.

The technician swipes across the tablet, activating the remaining dark grey mechs. Each mech retrieves its armaments from the weapon rack and lines up on the yellow-striped firing line. With another swipe, a crevice in the floor reveals six additional steel torso targets. In a perfectly coordinated display of destructive power, the mechs lock onto their targets, take aim, and unleash a barrage of fire. The steel surfaces of the targets become dimpled and pockmarked with silver craters, showcasing remarkable precision.

Suddenly, the crevice ejects a volley of glossy white ceramic saucers, sending them soaring in different directions, each reaching twenty feet into the air. The mechs react instantly, acquiring each new target and firing with incredible speed, powered by pneumatic pistons and servos. They seem to communicate silently through a wireless network, as each mech targets and eliminates a separate saucer, turning the discs into a shower of porcelain shards that rain down onto the floor below.

"Carbon-based service members, please hang up your boots and meet your replacements." The lead technician can't contain his excitement, letting out a whoop that echoes through the space. Darby rolls his eyes, checks his watch, and offers a half-hearted wave of approval to the lead technician before heading toward Pod B.

POD B 09:26:45 - 09/02/22
- Security Camera + Docu - Biomechatronics Lab, Pod B
- Primate Integration- Laboratory Documentation Camera- Laboratory Employee BodyCams

A balding, overweight middle-aged scientist wearing glasses adjusts his mustard-stained lab coat and straightens his posture for the camera, wiping back the few strands of hair he has left. The text appears on screen above his head: "G. Olsen - Supervising Lab Tech, Biomechatronics." His younger, shorter counterpart, "J. Dennard, Lab Tech, Biomechatronics," operates the handheld documentation camera.

"Joby, how does this look? I want to make sure I look good for the military guys during the reviews and stuff," Gil says, mustering as much confidence as he can for the camera lens.

"Oh yeah, you look official, Gil. Super legit, dude. Maybe just change your coat before they come, though," Joby replies.

"Of course! My mom did the laundry and ironed my good coat yesterday. It was pretty wrecked after last week's mishap..."

"Oh, right. That was a lot of blood," Joby quips.

"Okay, let's rehearse for the camera again so I can see how it looks now that we have the big stars of our presentation all linked up," Gil says anxiously as the camera zooms out and follows him deeper into the Pod, revealing a long wall of steel cages.

Most of the cages house chimpanzees, who stare curiously at their human stewards as they pass by. As the camera tracks their movement, some of the chimps begin vocalizing and rattling the steel doors, reaching through the bars to get attention. The camera angle, prepared by the arbiters on screen, starts to automatically switch between the handheld camera, the security cameras for Pod B, and the two affixed personal documentation cameras clipped to each scientist's lab coat lapel, showcasing their individual perspectives.

A glistening stainless steel operating table outfitted with securing straps sits beneath a high-intensity surgical light fixture. The floor slopes slightly toward a generous drainage grate beneath the table, surrounded by high-tech surgical apparatus, diagnostic equipment, and hinged robotic surgical arms suspended from ceiling mounts. High-tech meets highly industrial.

Gil speaks into an intercom microphone mounted on his lapel. "Alright, team, bring in Gary."

A moment later, three other scientists in surgical protective gear wheel in a gurney with the subject of the moment. Beneath a crisp white bedsheet lies a sedated adult male chimp, with wire leads taped to his upper chest and temple connected to a small portable vitals monitor. Gil turns to Joby's camera and gestures toward the primate as his team begins to transfer him to the steel operating table.

"Here we have Gary, a seven-year-old male chimpanzee. Gary has undergone a surgical amputation; his right arm was severed above the elbow and below the glenohumeral joint," Gil states proudly, demonstrating his rehearsed professional cadence.

On screen, we see that Gary indeed lacks an arm, replaced by a dull metallic sleeve covering the stump and a portion of shaved, raw reddish skin surrounding it. The team of masked surgeons gently removes the bedsheet and secures Gary's three intact limbs to the gurney with straps. One surgeon extends the articulating surgical table arm and elevates Gary's amputated arm, securing it, while another checks the chimp's vitals. The last lab technician inserts an IV line into Gary's intact arm. In the background, Darby enters an observation room separated by a glass partition, motions for Gil to continue, and begins texting on his cellphone, seemingly oblivious to the work being done on the other side.

The sliding door at the back of the room glides open and a young Indian-American female scientist, "Dr. Anika Das" approaches, holding a folder in hand. She approaches Gil and presents a packet of information.

"Dr. Gil, here's the updated neural-load readouts for you, sir.

Gil looks slightly annoyed as he takes the packet and flips through the chart.

"Yes, yes. Anika, I told you this is all within acceptable thresholds. Can't you see we're in the middle of a vlog here?" Gil says dismissively.

"But sir, the last session showed some levels were above the thresh-"

she begins before Gil waves her away.

"No worries, Anika. Moving on." Gil says as he motions her off and regains his composure for camera. She bows her head and walks off, dejected.

"Always with the damn threshold readings. Now, as I was saying before the interruption, for the camera and for the demonstration later this evening, can you tell us what we're doing and the technical procedure name, Gil?" Joby prompts.

"Ah, yes. Today, we are demonstrating the augmented synthetic limb assignments we've developed, coupled with the neural integration link. In layman's terms, our chimpanzee subject, Gary, will be showcasing his tools, and I will connect with him via the VR neural interface to 'pilot' him in surrogate control mode. Gary is one of our top students and excels in interfacing aptitude scoring, with zero cerebral rejections so far," Gil explains before breaking his presentation cadence to address Joby directly. "Of course, I won't mention it during the actual demo, but I received an official memo just before you arrived stating that we are reverting to chimpanzees for all of this quarter's tests because the gelada baboons were deemed…" Gil nervously chuckles, recalling something unpleasant, "…'inviable for this pilot program selection.' In other words, those little guys were going wild every time we made the cerebral link and were tearing each other - and our colleagues - apart. The remaining misbehavers are now slated for 'stress testing' in the Directed Energy Weapons division this month. Good riddance."

"Yeah, good riddance indeed. Blast them into oblivion," Joby mutters from behind his camera, still focused on Gil.

"Waste not, want not, when it comes to valuable testing inventory." Gil chuckles.

"Those mean little bastards are going to feel some heat, alright. Serves them right for what they did to Emily. I sort of liked her…" Joby adds, a touch of melancholy in his voice as he recalls an unpleasant recent memory.

"Yes, yes, young Joby. She'll be back up and walking again in no time; the company is taking care of her recovery. But alas, back to the task at hand," Gil says as he approaches the surgical table and examines Gary, the sedated chimp whose eyes are now rolling open, struggling to gain clarity and presence through a glassy gaze. The chimp manages to meet the fat man's eyes.

Gil points to the metallic cup encasing Gary's severed limb.

Protruding from the flat bottom of the metal underside are a series of small ports - recesses with finely machined locking quick-disconnect mounts.

"We've fully integrated the bio-magnetic QD mounts here, which I am personally very proud of. This allows for rapid replacement and swap-out of the available appendages, an aspect that has been a collaborative effort between divisions, I might add. Shout out to our colleagues in directed energy and the team down in the fabrication shop," Gil says as he simulates a celebratory gesture of "blowing it up" with his own two hands. He quickly pulls back a sheet on a nearby supply cart to reveal a number of finely manufactured mechanical appendages.

"Well, hello there!" Joby says excitedly from behind the camera as his buddy Gil reveals the selections.

The camera slowly pans over the hardware. The first appendage looks like a sharp crab's claw that might be used for heavy industrial lifting or some sort of mining or rescue operations. The next appears to be a facsimile of the primate's original arm, modeled to scale, stripping away unnecessary flesh and leaving only articulating mechanical joints made of what appears to be a dark carbon fiber-textured material, with black synthetic strands tethering the finger joints in place of ligaments and tendons. The third and final mechanical appendage appears to be more delicate in design, featuring a long copper rod at its center, surrounded by thinner protrusions of diamond-shaped angular metal coiling down its length, all interconnected further with thin copper wires curling in a vortex-style wrap.

"Not too shabby, right?" Gil says excitedly before launching into his presentation. "We've got something for everyone here, folks." He gestures first at the crab pincer. "Here we have the trusty 'Claw.' Not a very creative name, I know, but that's what happens when a bunch of engineers get together and are given naming rights. It's a 3D printed graphene-titanium alloy hybrid with diamond-coated bezels along the blades, and well, it claws stuff. It's like the jaws of life on roids. This thing could chomp through a Buick like it was made of marshmallows. But next, we have a real work of art: the synth-limb." Gil gestures to the sophisticated-looking arm and hand made from a skeletonized carbon fiber. "In brief, it's a super strong synthetic replacement for subjects experiencing catastrophic injury - ergo, lost limbs." Gil holds up the arm for Joby's camera to get a closer look.

"Very nice. Now, good doctor, tell us about the shocking

development over here," Joby says, encouraging his buddy as the handheld camera pans to the next selection.

"Oh yes. Here we have Nikola. I named it myself, and this one's my favorite. This guy taps into the power cell we have integrated into their bio-packs, and it can compound-generate about thirty thousand amps of directed juice toward a target, or multiple targets, without negatively affecting the operator. Clearing cluttered buildings or arcing around blind corners on a battlefield is no sweat with this guy."

"Well, shall we?!" Joby asks, clearly in excited anticipation.

"Yes, team. Let's wake up Gary here and start the linking process. Let's hook him up with the synth limb first," Gil instructs his staff, who immediately get to work administering a serum to Gary via an IV. The chimp awakens from the administration of the drug and becomes increasingly aware of his surroundings, while one of the technicians checks the dilation of his pupils with a small penlight, and another connects the synthetic limb by twisting and locking it into place with a swift snapping sound. As the limb joins with the primate's metallic stump, Gary, instantly attuned to his new extension, raises his eyebrows and turns his full attention to his now articulating synthetic fingers, flexing and stretching them while rolling the wrist joint.

"Excellent, we have connection, team. Okay, now it's time for the fun part," Gil says as he unveils what appears to be a pair of visually identical, streamlined VR headsets mounted to ballistic helmets via the Wilcox mount typically used to affix night vision. The only difference between the two VR helmets is that one has a small tail of colorful coiled cables protruding from the rear. The lab technicians take this particular headset over to Gary, while Gil holds up the other for the camera to see. In the background, it looks like the lab techs are administering eye drops to Gary, who flinches and turns his head in irritation during the process. "Once I link up with Gary via the neural network integration, I will have control of the little fuzzball, like piloting him in a video game." Gil breaks his presenter voice and looks to the left of the camera at Joby. "Don't you think it's better to just show them during this part?"

"Yeah, agreed. Cut to the chase," Joby affirms.

Gil nods and swiftly dons the helmet, lowering the attached VR headset. Comical in appearance while wearing the tactical-style helmet, he bears no resemblance to a mercenary of any sort. The VR headset adds a huge geek factor, making him look instead like a hybrid between a basement gamer and an overweight airsoft enthusiast obsessed with *Call of Duty* video games.

"Does this look cool? Don't lie, dude," Gil asks earnestly of his trusted compatriot, Joby.

"Oh… dude… totally, man, I mean, you look really… tactical," Joby says, trying earnestly to mask his embellishment.

"Excellent," Gil says confidently.

A sharp crackle tears through the intercom overhead, startling them both. Darby's impatient voice rings out across the pod, like a nagging god overhead. "I don't have all day, Gil. Get on with it. I still have to visit the rest of the division."

The camera whip pans over to Darby, knocking on the glass divider and impatiently tapping his wristwatch as he watches them from afar.

"Got it! Okay, no sweat, Mr. Darby!" Gil yells back blindly, giving the thumbs-up sign in the general direction of the observation area where Darby is watching.

Joby quickly refocuses the camera on the laboratory technicians in the background as they place the other headset on Gary and secure it with a series of rugged-looking straps. One of the techs hand-feeds Gary a small treat as a reward for behaving so well. The chimp looks like he enjoys the treat as they lower the VR visor over his eyes. In fact, and perhaps more aptly a matter of routine, Gary the chimp doesn't seem distressed during this process but merely curious about his situation and the behavior of his human counterparts.

The camera moves closer to the action as the techs delicately unravel the bundled nest of cables extending from the helmet and reach around to the backside of Gary's head. The camera zooms in on a small shaved patch within his otherwise thick black hair that reveals a small metallic port, surgically implanted and leading directly into the base of Gary's skull. With a swift motion, the jack end of the cable's pigtail switch is inserted and clicked into a locked position, and Gary goes completely limp on the gurney in an instant. Simultaneously, Gil sways, as if his balance was disrupted, and he quickly steadies himself. He gestures with both hands in the air before Gary suddenly sits upright.

"Wow, there it is. Connection," Gil exclaims, raising his arm and flexing his fingers. In perfect sync, Gary the chimp raises his mechanical arm and mimics the same gesture with its dexterous hinged "fingers." Gil giggles to himself, then points to the air, then to the floor, and back to the air, prompting Gary to echo his best impression of John Travolta from *Saturday Night Fever*. Joby laughs behind the camera.

Intercut: CAMERA ANGLE - PRIMATE VISOR POV / HUD - 4K, 120FPS and Lab Documentation DSLR CameraContinued. 09:45:57

From Gary the chimp's perspective, we see the room ahead. Amid flashes of furry arms performing disco dance moves, we catch glimpses of Gil mirroring the actions while wearing the VR control headset, looking back at the primate. The view from Gary's visor displays Gil in a mirrored perspective through the neural link, miming hand gestures as Gary echoes his movements in perfect synchronization. Gil studies his remote-controlled subject intently, gazing into the chimp's face on his HUD, creating a VR paradox akin to staring at yourself in a double-mirrored funhouse, caught in an infinite loop. Meanwhile, Joby stands nearby with a handheld DSLR camera, panning between the two and documenting the bizarre trance.

"Alright, time to unleash the beast, team," Gil announces, "Here we go..."

Gary swiftly moves across the floor as Gil communicates with a series of rapid hand gestures - a blend of sign language and mystical commands guiding the chimp's movements. Gary strides purposefully to a door and pulls it open. Beyond lies another gymnasium outfitted with high parallel bars, stair steps, climbing walls, and staggered scaffolding. Through Gary's eyes, the dizzying speed and bouncing camera movements capture his sprinting, leaping, and bounding up the nearest set of steps. Once atop a twenty-foot platform, the chimp, piloted by Gil, lunges and grabs on to a suspended bar, hanging and surveying the space. Finally, the POV shifts down through the glass observation wall of Pod B, revealing Darby looking up at the VR headset-wearing Gary. Darby, now intrigued by the display beyond the glass, pushes aside the team of technicians in the observation room for a better view of the vertical gymnasium beyond.

CAMERA ANGLE - POD B - LAB

"The remote-controlled apes are a great start. How are we looking for full integration with the neural link in our human test subjects?" Darby asks Joby.

"Eh... the appendage synthesis is good to go. But every time we attempt a full link with the human test subjects, they melt down and go psychotic for a day whenever their sense of self is reintroduced. We haven't fully or officially diagnosed it, but it's like the brain rejects its own original operating software, then overloads the pain centers until they hyperventilate and black out," Joby says, grimacing at the uneasy thought.

"Just show me," Darby replies impatiently.

POD C - 09:53:57 - 09/02/22

Intercut: Security Camera - Biomechatronics Lab, Pod C, Human NeuraLink- Laboratory Documentation Camera and Laboratory Employee BodyCams

Darby and Joby enter the sterile lab together. A female lab technician wearing full surgical scrubs and a face shield is standing at a reclined surgical chair, taking the vitals of a muscular man wearing only a surgical gown and a web of prison tattoos that lace his entire body - everywhere but on his mechanical right arm.

"Mr. Darby would like us to demo a full integration link-up sequence," Joby instructs the technician.

"But, sir, I thought we were to refrain - " the technician begins before Joby quickly dismisses her with a wave.

"Just do it. Make sure to dose him first; hopefully, it will help take the edge off the comeback," Joby instructs curtly. The lab technician looks weary but complies, injecting the test subject in his real arm with a syringe of fluid. The man's shoulders visibly relax, and he takes a deep breath as the sedation from whatever he was just administered takes quick effect. The technician grabs a small black box from a nearby surgical tray, which has a small cable protruding from it, similar to the one used to connect to Gary the chimp. She quickly clips it onto an area at the back of the man's head, near the base of his skull.

"Was he a soldier? Did he lose the arm in the war?" Darby asks, half interested, gesturing to the test subject's missing arm.

Joby pulls up a nearby tablet and swipes it to find the answer in the man's bio. He smiles. "Nah. Just a convict from the exchange program. Lost the arm in a prison riot, according to the file," Joby says.

"Huh... Well, thanks for your service anyway. Let's get on with it." Darby chuckles to himself. Joby nods to the nearby technician, who connects the cable leading from the small black box into the port on the back of the test subject's skull. The man jolts once and then settles back into the reclined steel chair. Joby holds up the tablet for Darby to see their own images appearing via the POV being fed from the test subject's own eyes.

"So, the initial link process has been successful for the last few months. Super stable feed, and we worked out the bugs on long-distance connections by using the StarNet satellites. We can even manipulate beyond basic gross motor skills and control navigation pretty well," Joby says as he swipes through a few entries on the tablet. The test subject jerks and moves both methodically and mechanically up and out of the chair. After some effort and careful balancing, the man stabilizes himself into a fully upright standing position. It's like watching a toddler learning to walk use a couch for support before taking calculated steps... or Frankenstein's Monster maneuvering the laboratory after being brought back to life for the first time.

"Okay, so we have liftoff. We could make him do anything we want, right? Arm him to the teeth, drop him off on target, blast everyone and everything that gets in its way? Mission accomplished, right?" Darby asks, chuckling to himself.

"Well... the problem is, we're still working out a few minor issues," Joby says, frowning.

"What is it?" Darby inquires, genuinely interested.

"Well, beyond the reintegration thing I mentioned, they also do this any time they see their own reflection." Joby swipes a command on the tablet and begins tracing his finger on the screen, guiding the test subject's movement. The tattooed subject marches in a half-drunk waddle, dragging his slippers along the tile floor with each labored step. He trucks along dutifully until he approaches a nearby bank of polished stainless steel refrigeration units. The moment he gets close enough to see his own reflection, his spine stiffens, and his movements become ragged. Although still in motion to walk forward, the subject's gaze strains and appears intensified, conflicted even, with his eyes fixed on the reflective steel surfaces. His gait shudders as he locks his eyes fully onto the smooth, mirrored surface of the refrigerator. His expression goes cold, then twists with primal rage. He screams and raises his mechanical fist in a shaky, labored motion, as if fighting his own will against the direction commanded by Joby's hand. Then, abruptly, he bashes himself in the face. Blood spurts from his crumpled nose. Another swift blow from the bludgeoning, piston-driven mechanical arm concaves his cheekbone and eye socket as well. He collapses to the floor and begins convulsing, writhing on the ground, his feet flailing and mechanical arm twisting and gripping at nothing.

The bolted-on appendage goes haywire as it knocks his natural limbs into the nearby equipment. Darby startles and steps back, watching in macabre amusement.

"Dose him again and disconnect!" Joby instructs the female lab tech without offering any assistance. She hastily grabs a nearby syringe and dodges the man's thrashing limbs to jab it into his neck, depressing the plunger in the process. The man's convulsions instantly steady. Moments later, he lies completely limp on the shiny floor as blood pools around his head. A door glides open nearby, and two other surgical gear-clad lab technicians enter the room with a gurney, scoop up the test subject, and take him away as if he were merely a spill on aisle five in the supermarket that just needed to be cleaned up. Joby and Darby both take a deep breath, shaking their heads at the crimson streak left on the floor.

"Like I said. A few bugs to work out." Joby says, frowning.

"Jesus... Well, I think we'll stick with the chimps today," Darby mutters, shaking his head in disgust. "How are the guys in the wet lab coming along?"

"Oh, they're good. They're working on some cool shit over there, for sure." Joby nods in admiration.

Camera cuts to:

10:03:12 - 09/02/22

Security Cameras, Lanes 1-4: Directed Energy Lab, Testing Range / Wet Lab

Chiseled deep into the mountain's core, the dark, glistening, gutted slick granite interior is lit with bright rows of industrial LED tube lights. Extending deep into the length of the cavernous space are a dozen individually sectioned lanes, each separated by waist-high concrete barricades running the entire depth of the area, and topped with ten-foot-tall polycarbonate glass panes. It resembles an indoor shooting range on a massive scale, with each lane bearing distance markings painted on the ground every ten yards and outfitted with different types of targets at varied distances. These targets do not appear as steel silhouettes or paper targets with concentric bullseyes; instead, they seem to be exclusively organic matter-based.

A live goat stands downrange, chained to a pole embedded in the ground at the twenty-five-yard marker in lane number 1. The animal mindlessly chews on some cud as one of the facility's many lab-coated technicians roams throughout the area, stepping up to a shooting bench fixed behind the firing line. From beneath the bench, the technician retrieves a long metallic cylinder that resembles a large industrial fire extinguisher. This device, however, has two rubberized contoured grips on each side with red engagement triggers protruding from their undersides and push-button ignitions extending from the top of each corresponding handle. An intricate web of metallic tubing curls toward a series of interlinked vacuum tube fixtures set along the length of the gleaming cylinder.

The technician works around the device, securing it within a cradle fixture bolted to the top of the bench and looping a steel ratchet strap around it to hold it firmly in place. He examines his placement and alignment with the target before nodding in approval. Then, he pulls a thick electrical cable from a rack of cable reels at a nearby station, extending enough length to reach his table. Pulling on a pair of welding goggles, he plugs and twists the thick male end of the cable into a receptacle at the rear of the cylinder. With the flip of a switch embedded on the side of the device, literal lightning in a bottle sparks into existence in front of the tech, reflecting wildly off the dark glass of his goggles. Brilliant tiny arcs of electricity sparkle and crackle as they weave their way throughout the glass tubes.

The industrial room lights mounted to the ceiling and surrounding lanes begin to flicker and dim slightly. A faint humming sound rises in volume on camera in relation to the increasing flow of electricity being channeled and harnessed within the device. Soon, the entire body of the device glows flame-orange. The technician bends down, steadying himself behind the electrically charged device while peering intently downrange over the top of the apparatus. Tentatively, he grips the two side handles with rubber-gloved hands and aims downrange using a holographic reflex sight mounted on top of the device. Satisfied with the acquired target and trajectory, he depresses the triggers on each curved handhold and simultaneously pushes each ignition switch with his thumbs.

A deafening crack reverberates through the cavern as a violent discharge of lightning bolts erupts from the device, streaking downrange. The electricity appears chaotic, fracturing and wildly flickering as it tears down the shooting range lane, with strands of energy peeling off and reconnecting along its path. Despite this frenzy, the central beam of electricity remains focused squarely on its target. When the tip of the central electric stream finally strikes the goat, the fractal arcs converge at the point of contact like blinding needles, igniting the goat's hair and flesh instantaneously. A brilliant flash momentarily reveals the silhouette of the shocked animal at the heart of the searing lightning storm. Its legs stiffen, muscles spasming and locking, while arcs of lightning pulse steadily from the technician's firing bench in a crackling stream of energy.

Amidst the swirling smoke, the goat emits an unnaturally high-pitched trill accompanied by a popping sound as its insides rupture, spilling onto the floor in a steaming heap. Gravity soon pulls what remains of the goat down to the hard stone floor. The surging arcs of electricity abruptly cut off, and the animal's convulsions are barely visible through the smoke and flames consuming its charred remains. The sound of escaping gas comes from deep within the goat's belly, which twitches and smokes, its skin blistering and popping like an overcooked pizza. An industrial exhaust fan activates overhead, drawing in the smoke and fumes, followed by a sharp burst of fire suppression gas to extinguish the remaining flames. As the haze clears on the screen, only a charred and blackened husk, resembling a goat with protruding horns and smoking hooves, remains amidst the ash.

In Lane 2, the plight of animal rights is no better. A screeching gelada baboon is strapped to an upright stainless steel table, its limbs - including a mechanical leg - pulled outward into an "X" shape. As it twists and writhes against its bindings, its vocalizations echo off the granite walls, resembling an army of apes marching deep within the mountain. The baboon is determined not to go quietly. At the firing line, another technician, clad in a lab coat, thick padded thermal gloves, and eye protection, carefully manipulates metal tongs to place a freezing vial into a circular receptacle atop a large, rectangular rifle. Instead of a conventional barrel, a three-pronged claw-like fixture extends from the business end of the odd-looking gun. After securing the vial and closing the lid, the technician shoulders the rifle, activates a priming safety switch, and aims downrange. Charging indicator bars light up along the length of the rifle, glowing pale blue. Once fully illuminated, they turn pale green, signaling that the rifle is primed. The talon-shaped barrel begins to spin, and almost instantly, three small bluish-purple orbs of plasma ignite at the tips of the talon prongs, undulating like jellyfish made of pure condensed particle energy. As the glowing orbs spin faster, they blur into a circular streak of blue-purple light. The technician flicks a red safety switch to the firing-enabled position, aims downrange, and squeezes the trigger.

The plasma rifle recoils heavily as the orbs of energy shoot from the taloned barrel in a flash. At normal speed, the camera doesn't capture the energy orbs' dance around one another, orbiting in rapid corkscrew loops as they accelerate toward their target. However, when played in slow motion, the Junior Arbiters' playback reveals this dynamic movement, prompting our division to note this accomplishment in the overall report. Interesting.

As the plasma orbs approach the baboon, its screeching crescendos, passing the five-yard line and entering the end zone. Upon contact, the baboon's expression shifts from rage to agony. Straining against its restraints, it twists its long face, baring its angry jaw, pink gums, and extended canine teeth. Its bellows and final reproach are muffled, drowned out by the loud, slapping sound of atmosphere being chewed. The beauty of the plasma orbs in slow motion unfolds dramatically as they strike organic matter, unleashing a violent bio-fusion reaction. The plasma spheres first latch on to, then meld with the baboon's body, simultaneously melting its internal and external structures. In a cacophonous flash, the baboon is radiated externally while being boiled from within, the energy penetrating and expanding through its body like a mini supernova. The incineration of hair, flesh, bone, and entrails culminates in a blast, sending blood, bits of organs, clumps of fur, and fragments of bone and teeth flying from a black cloud of ash, splattering across Lanes 1, 2, 3, and 4 as if a bloody water grenade had exploded. The cycle of cellular destruction completes, leaving only twitching limbs and tightly curled paws hanging from the binding apparatus in Lane 2.

In Lane 3, the cold, blue-lipped corpse of another tattooed subject is strapped to an upright steel gurney. On the Lane 3 firing line table rests a conventional high-powered air rifle equipped with a scope. A lab technician prepares a syringe filled with thick yellowish fluid to load into the rifle. After ensuring the dart is chambered correctly, the technician swiftly raises the rifle, flicks off the safety, and fires the dart downrange. The syringe strikes the corpse directly in the chest with a dull thud. For a moment, there are no visible effects, but soon the corpse's chest and abdomen begin to ripple. Initially, the movement is slow, but it escalates into a rolling spasm, the pale bluish skin undulating as something churns beneath the surface. Fumes begin to escape from the mouth and nostrils, dark pink vapor pouring from the orifices. Before long, it is as if the very structure of bone and cartilage within the corpse collapses in on itself.

From the point of impact, the corpse's bone structure appears to liquefy, the neck and head flopping like a loose mask of skin, while the eyeballs and tongue evacuate their sockets. As the rib cage dissolves and the legs transform into long strands of skin, a liquid emulsion of blood, guts, bile, excrement, liquefied bone, and fat floods onto the dark granite floor from every open orifice. The camera angle cuts.

10:11:37 - 09/02/22
Security Camera - Organic Materials Lab

The security camera captures a view of the lab, where several massive windowed riveted steel tanks line the walls. In the center of the room, four open-topped vats filled with glowing teal liquid illuminate the space with ripples of bluish light. A single scientist, clad in a respirator and a full hazmat suit, walks between the rows of glowing fluid, peering into each vat and jotting notes on a clipboard. The scene is surprisingly serene. However, as they move down the row, something floats by in one of the large windowed tanks, obscuring the light within. It's murky and swift, but the long serpentine shape clearly maneuvers in front of one of the vat windows before turning sharply and disappearing into the haze of the liquid. An aquatic creature, perhaps?

The camera quickly cuts between several angles. This editing technique is routine; Junior Arbiters often compile footage for review in this manner to maintain a timeline and reference point for key players in the overall sequence of events being evaluated. It also provides a secondary layer of review, allowing us to catch details that the initial teams may have missed. This method of review is known within Memory Lane as "breadcrumb cuts."

10:13:15
Security Camera - Temporal Lab, Observation and Control Room

Dr. Turner works diligently at his terminal, pausing only briefly to remove his glasses and rub his tired eyes before returning to his tasks. Li Meng stands behind him, looking over his shoulder at a series of charts and readout displays on his monitor. Nearby, Davies sips a can of Red Bull while listening to music through his earbuds. Dr. Turner appears exhausted and frustrated as he leans back in his chair, trying to make sense of the computer data.

"Every simulation has been within parameters for months, and then, of all days, we get one that pops." Li places a hand on his shoulder and squeezes, her gesture seeming more than just friendly. "Ninety-nine point nine, nine, nine percent of the simulations have been stable out of billions, and you're worrying over an anomalous model projection that you pushed beyond the edge of probability on purpose. It's going to hold; you know it will."

Dr. Turner places his hand over hers and looks up at her over his glasses. "I know. We've only used Element 115 once, at half-thrust. I just don't want to leave anything to chance. After all, this is one of the few places in the world where theoretical physics meets practical application." He runs his hands through his hair, pausing to consider deeply before saying, "Let's run the full spectrum probability model one more time."

Li takes a deep breath, then nods and walks to her terminal to begin making entries. The screens clear, and a new model simulation boots up on the screen. "Okay, one more... if it will make you feel better," she says. These two clearly have a deeper relationship outside the lab. Li is in love with her mentor...

10:15:39
Security Camera - Office - Charles Darby, Site Management

Charles Darby has retired to his large personal office, which more closely resembles a swanky Manhattan high-rise apartment loft., Dressed only in his boxer shorts, wife beater undershirt, and tennis shoes with calf high socks, he sweats profusely and is beet red in the face as he plods along brutishly on an elliptical trainer at quite the aggressive clip for a man not in peak physical condition. Taking a greedy swig from a can of Diet Coke, it appears that he is exercising his professional demons, as it were, grumbling to himself angrily and punctuating every loping and swooshing step with profanity. "Fucking bullshit. Call me and fuckin' - tell me that my - ass is on the line. - Shit ass fuckers in New York - while I've been in this - shitty town for nine - shitty months. - Dickhead scientist pricks - blowing the time budget. - Not me! Missing deadlines. - Fucking bullshit." He pedals furiously as if trying to escape his situation, escape the lab, escape period.

10:15:40 - 18:11:54 09/02/22

Security Camera - Exterior - West Entrance Point Delta / Helipad

The security camera, mounted high above the reinforced steel blast doors, offers a panoramic view of the desert stretching for miles. The lab's west-facing entrance, embedded into the mountainside, opens to a long walkway of reinforced concrete, lined with blinking lights. This walkway extends directly from the massive blast door and is flanked by thick steel cable guard rails, running between two heavy, electronically locked security gates at either end. These gates serve as checkpoints between the walkway and the bridge leading to the helipad, located approximately forty yards from the blast door entrance. Beyond the helipad is a sheer drop-off the mountain's cliff face. Suddenly, the footage accelerates into a time-lapse, capturing the orange sun moving steadily across the sky toward the western horizon. As it sets, it casts long, stretching shadows over the helipad and the valley below. A few thin white stratus clouds drift across the azure sky, tapering off and dissolving. The timecode rapidly speeds up, and the hues of sunset begin to emerge, with shades of orange, deep red, and finally purple dominating the southwestern sky.

8

The footage abruptly resumes normal speed. The illuminated landing markers surrounding the helipad start to flash, while a series of mounted industrial lights illuminate the large "H" painted on the concrete. A deep clanking sound, followed by the grinding and metallic movement of gears and pistons, precedes the massive steel blast door slowly recessing into the mountainside. Moments later, Darby, now dressed in his suit and tie, strides outside, closely followed by a group of laboratory technicians struggling to keep pace. He navigates the walkway, using his keycard to open both security checkpoint gates along the way. Darby stops at the helipad, looking expectantly at the horizon and pointing at something off-camera to his team. The sound of an approaching helicopter becomes clearly audible. Darby glances back at the team, ensuring he stands prominently at the front and center, irritably urging some of them to step back before returning his gaze to the sky. A moment later, a Blackhawk helicopter descends toward the helipad, its rotor wash stirring up dust as it adjusts its pitch slightly, raising its nose just before landing smoothly on the pad. Darby does his best to maintain composure and a welcoming grin, but the wind and dust wreak havoc on his hair and relentlessly slap his tie against his face. As the rotors begin to wind down, Darby quickly moves to greet their guests, ducking low and hurrying to the helicopter door.

The helicopter's side door slides open, and General Dennings steps out, dressed in full regalia and heavily decorated. Standing at six feet seven inches, the stoic African American general appears larger than life, accentuated by Darby's shorter stature as he ducks to avoid the rotors. Once clear of the helicopter, General Dennings stands at attention, surveying the landing pad and his greeters. The frame freezes, and text appears on screen above the towering military man, verifying the General's identity from his personnel file:

PERSONNEL: - GENERAL JOSEPH DENNINGS: 4 STAR: US ARMY 1984 - PRESENT. VERIFIED.

The video resumes playback.

Following the general is his escort of heavily armed security. Unlike a typical transport or off-site visit, this group of six soldiers appears out of place alongside a high-ranking general. Their worn fatigues, customized automatic weapons, lack of formal unit insignias, and abundance of facial hair suggest they are likely US Special Forces. The video freezes again, and text appears.

SUPPORT PERSONNEL IDs: UNVERIFIED. CONFIRMATION PROCESSING.

The absence of readily available intel indicates these operatives had their digital footprints scrubbed by one of the frontline agencies, and it is impressive yet ultimately futile, as our team will inevitably identify them. Given the facility they are visiting, these heavily armed operators are presumably former Delta members with multiple aliases, now working as contractors under whatever pseudonym they have adopted. From experience, my deduction is that these are highly skilled and seasoned operators known for their moral flexibility and uncanny ability to remain anonymous for the right price. Regardless of their identities, it will only be a matter of hours before our team in the Hive uncovers their significance in the unfolding story. The video playbook resumes.

Two of the muscular security detail visibly strain as they lift a small, cooler-sized metallic crate from the Blackhawk and gently place it onto the helipad. Whatever is inside must be heavy, as evidenced by their effort to set it atop a small industrial roller dolly that a third member of their team carefully unpacks, unfolds, and slides beneath it.

"General, it's great to see you again. I'm excited for today's big demonstration and to show you some of the more…terrestrial developments we've been working on for you and the boys in the sandbox. But first, would you and your team like something to drink, perhaps to refresh before we start the tour?" Darby extends his hand to shake the General's but is met with a cold gaze.

"I am on a tight timeline and do not expect this visit to extend any longer than scheduled, Mr. Darby."

"Of course, of course. Cutting right to the chase as usual; that's what I like to hear. You're a man who appreciates efficiency as much as I do."

"As per our arrangement, I have brought the necessary payload for the experiment and would like to relay my word to Washington by this evening regarding any continued commitments to the program."

Darby quickly adjusts himself and gestures for the blast door, slowly moving to guide the General and his team inside. Everything about the General is disciplined and mission-focused down to his stance, his gait, his stone-walled face, and his no-nonsense approach to executing the task at hand. In contrast, Darby's attempts at glad-handing, small talk, and general white-collar bullshit is met quite clearly with disinterest by the General.

"That's the kind of go-get'em attitude I like to see in our future Secretary of Defense. I hear that it's looking good for your appointment, by the way," Darby says as the General rolls his eyes, knowing when he's being flattered and played. "So, let's get the show on the road, then, shall we?"

Darby starts to pick up his stride, remaining in lockstep with the General as they move down the bridge toward the blast door. Then, he stops abruptly, squaring up as best as he can with the towering figure of the General before him.

"But of course, before we enjoy the main attraction, I did promise our special mutual friends with benefits in Washington that you'd give our secondary programs a quick review. The tour has already been paid for, if you get my drift, so please, just do me the honor? You know how the DC squares are about following their orders…"

General Dennings looks down his nose at Darby, bristling at the tone and approach. Darby just grins his shit-eating grin back at him. "It won't take any more time than allotted, I promise, and I think you'll enjoy it. Besides, Doctor Turner isn't even going to be ready to integrate the special package here into the reactor for about half an hour..." Darby says as he gently pats the metallic crate.

The General looks increasingly annoyed, but motions for his soldiers to move ahead into the building with the package. "Fine. Let's get it done. Move out," General Dennings orders his team.

Four of the soldiers from the detachment proceed, with two of them pushing the small container along on the dolly cart toward the blast doors. Two other soldiers escort General Dennings with their weapons slung low and ready as they scan the mountain face and perimeter while moving swiftly into the glowing interior of the mountain complex. Darby scurries behind them, following closely on their heels with his gaggle of lab coats in tow behind.

The footage again plays in a timelapse as the night sky and stars overhead on the horizon shift and rotate.

9

Security Cameras, Lane 2: Directed Energy Lab, Testing Range /
Wet Lab

Darby escorts the General and his entourage of Special Operators into
the test firing range. The blood, guts, and charred remains from
previous demonstrations have been cleaned up, and all the setups
Darby previewed during his walkabout are reset and ready for display.
Fresh test subjects are positioned downrange in their respective lanes:
a goat, a baboon, and a convict in a yellow jumpsuit. Up at the firing
line, advanced prototype weaponry is staged, while a dedicated
technician conducts final checks on each unit. A newly added table
hosts a lab technician wearing large noise-canceling earmuffs and a
substantial backpack apparatus. Two thick cables run from the pack to
a small silver handheld device resembling a satellite dish, which he
points downrange. Upon seeing Darby and the military detail enter,
the technician removes his protective gear and stands at attention.
"Oh, look at this!" Darby exclaims with jubilant enthusiasm. "I didn't
think this unit would be ready for today's demo! I'm really eager for
you to see this one - it's my favorite, the sonic dis - what are we calling
it now?" he asks the technician.

"Sonic Destabilizer," the technician replies. "It focuses a concentrated output of harmonic dissonance that obliterates the cellular walls of a subject - " Darby shoots him a glare for speaking out of turn and providing details unprompted. The technician quickly shuts his mouth and, a moment later, redirects, "What subject would you like on the line, sir?"

Darby grins and clasps his hands together, considering his options gleefully. "I mean, go big or go home, right, General? We have our VIPs here for a show after all. How are we looking on the good behavior pool? Do we have another one on deck?" he asks, gesturing toward the convict in the yellow jumpsuit downrange.

"We have two more on site. Real bad characters. I'll call one up right away, sir," the technician says eagerly, moving to a wall-mounted telephone.

Darby leans in to General Dennings. "Life sentence cons, violent offenders. We recently worked out a deal with one of the private prisons. You know how it is with all the red tape at the government level these days. Don't ask, don't tell, I say. They all think they're here for medical research... which isn't entirely untrue." Darby chuckles.

Dennings appears unimpressed but nods in understanding. The lab technician returns and distributes ear protection to each member of the visiting party. One of the Special Forces members scoffs at the earmuffs being offered.

"We really need those for that thing?" he asks, nodding toward the odd dish-shaped device while other squad members don the protective gear.

"Oh no, trust me. Unless you want spinal fluid leaking out your nose, you're going to want to wear those," Darby says as he puts on his own earmuffs. The soldier scowls but decides to heed the advice, putting on the protective equipment along with the rest of the personnel in the range.

10

Security Camera - Temporal Lab, Observation and Control Room

Dr. Turner paces the room, observing a series of colorful animated charts and visual projections dancing on the large display window.

"We'll run it incrementally, then do a deep scan at ninety percent, just to be safe..." Turner states. Davies spins in his chair and stands slowly, scratching his head in thought as he turns to Dr. Turner, looking nervous.

"Doc, look... last time, we lost stasis at eighty percent thrust. I know that most of the new models based on your modifications are looking stable, which makes sense since they're using the stabilized variant of the fuel for this one. But if we push it too far too fast, we risk - "

"I know the risk, Davies," Dr. Turner replies coldly. "The entire damn loop collapses, no success, and we're out of here. Done. That scenario has already been made clear by that shithead Darby. We all know the risk."

"I'm not worried about the professional collapse, Doc. I'm just saying, if the thrusters are firing at that rate and we can't shut it down..."

"I know the risk, Davies. I won't let that happen." Dr. Turner's tone leaves no room for further discussion.

Davies nods, turns back to his computer terminal, and begins inputting data dutifully. Li Meng stops typing, takes a deep breath, looks up at Dr. Turner, and then quickly returns to her work.

"Copy that, Doc. Ninety percent hold threshold." The young scientist's voice reveals a hint of reluctance, but his loyalty to Dr. Turner compels him to comply. His next words, captured on camera and amplified by the editorial team, would likely have been a mere mutter in the room: "I'll set my alarms, so if it edges close to a collapse, we can throttle it back before it becomes too dangerous."

Deep in thought, Dr. Turner intently reviews the animated charts and graph projections oscillating on the large observation window before him.

Li Meng bites her lip and presses her fingernails into her palms at her terminal, her visible stress mirroring that of her two colleagues.

"It will hold," Li speaks up, her tone self-assured yet clearly defensive, almost proud of Dr. Turner's steadfast assertion.

Turner steps forward, standing inches from the floor-to-ceiling window, gazing down into the adjacent lab that houses the massive machinery and testing equipment. The camera angle shifts to capture the scene, revealing several small figures in white lab coats working around the expansive particle accelerator and its connected machinery.

"Davies... page Darby. Let him know we'll be ready in thirty minutes. Also, alert the onboarding crew below to prepare," he commands defiantly before turning back to his two colleagues. "Li, walk with me; I need to clear my head."

19:58:47 09/02/22
   - Security Camera - Biomechatronics Lab, Pod B - Primate Integration

General Dennings and the Spec Ops team are visible from the high-security camera angle as Darby gives them a tour of the primate cages. Gary the chimp sits dutifully in a chair, wearing a VR visor, while a lab technician across from him conducts a test, mimicking hand motions to check the connectivity between their visors. The loudspeaker crackles to life.

"Paging Charles Darby, the temporal laboratory team will be ready in thirty minutes for the demo." General Dennings appears irritated as he checks his watch, continuing to follow Darby and the team on their tour. He briefly pauses to watch a chimpanzee mimic the lab technician's movements, scowls in disgust, and then rejoins the group as they move deeper into the lab.

20:02:06
   - Security Camera - Janitorial Supply Room

This camera, slightly obscured by a plastic jug of cleaning solution, is mounted in the far corner of the room. It captures dark footage using infrared in black and white. Industrial racks filled with bulk cleaning supplies and boxes line the shelving units. The room is completely still and quiet, except for one tall rack of supplies, which subtly rocks back and forth, creaking with each movement. Suddenly, the camera's microphone picks up the unmistakable groaning and grunting of Dr. Turner as he climaxes, exclaiming, "Oh…yes! …. Li…" to which Li responds with a squeal. Abruptly, the rocking of the supply shelf stops.

Moments later, Dr. Turner rounds the rack of supplies while buttoning his trousers. Li follows, snapping her shirt and adjusting her pants. Flushed, she spins around and kisses the doctor affectionately, then brushes the perspiration from his brow and gazes into his eyes adoringly.

"Better now?" she asks playfully.

"Much," he replies before returning her affection.

"Good. Now go in there and prove that jerk wrong. This is your chance to show the world what is possible," Li encourages in her best pep talk voice.

"Us. It's time for us to show the world what's possible, my love," he responds.

They kiss again before Dr. Turner carefully opens the supply room door and peers into the hallway to ensure it is clear. Confident that no one is around, they exit together.

11

Security Camera - Hallway A

Darby strides confidently down the hall at the front of the group, with General Dennings and his security detail closely behind.

"Aren't you glad we took the time to see the progress in biomechatronics? Impressive advancements, right? This should be great for the wounded warriors and all that..." Darby comments.

"I'll admit, Darby, some of the next-gen weapons show promise - if you can solve the remote power source issue. And nothing radioactive or highly experimental." The General glances down at the case on the roller dolly being pushed by his escort. "The last thing we need is some cave-dwelling extremist gutting one of those glorified ray guns for uranium or whatever else you're testing and making a dirty bomb to use against us."

"Uranium? No, of course not. We've been experimenting with a neutral fusion generation engine - " Darby starts to explain, but the General cuts him off sharply.

"Regardless. The robotics division is mildly intriguing. But I'll be damned if I'm going to sign off on pouring money into turning the planet of the goddamn apes into a battlefield. That side of the operation is a freak show," Dennings says, his contempt evident.

Darby forces a smile, stops at a doorway, retracts his security lanyard, and waves it over the magnetic keypad. The doorway whooshes open, and Dennings and his team move through briskly. Darby quickly matches their stride.

"I hear you, General, loud and clear. No skin off our backs. Uncle Sam is our number one VIP customer, after all. We're just the fantasy factory making new toys for the meat bags on the front lines. No offense, boys." Darby nods to the escort of hardened mercenaries. "If you decide to sample a little bit of what's on the main menu and leave some of the rest, it's all good. Whatever isn't gobbled up, I'm sure the DoD will pay us a fair fee to ensure we don't sell it off to the competition. Like you said, we wouldn't want any of it falling into the wrong hands," Darby says wryly, playing hardball now. The General seethes as he looks down his nose at the ferret-like man.

"Yes, I'm sure," Dennings manages, before grumbling, "Now show me what I actually came here for."

Security Camera - Temporal Lab, Observation and Control Room

Darby and the military personnel enter the room. Dr. Turner, Li Meng, and Davies turn away from their terminals and stand expectantly. Darby gestures to the floor.

"General, the team has been eager to present the demo to you. Dr. Turner assures me that this presentation will make the trip worthwhile. The floor is yours."

General Dennings strides up to Dr. Turner, who shakes his hand with respect. A clear rapport exists between the two men.

"Doctor, I look forward to seeing your progress. As you know, this program remains a primary interest for us. Unlike the other divisions we've just reviewed, this one has the potential to transform the battlefield on every level. However, we will allocate continued research funding to only one lab, and yours is among those in contention."

"This program has the potential to alter the world as we know it, General. I'm confident that my team's efforts will outshine those of the other labs, any day of the week," Dr. Turner replies matter-of-factly.

"You seem very confident, Doctor," General Dennings observes, admiring the man's determination.

"No ego, General. It's simply a fact of science. We've tested and proven better results. I look forward to demonstrating that to you." Dr. Turner glances at the heavy metallic case on the roller cart between the two mercenaries.

"Indeed. My men have the stabilized Element 115. Where would you like it placed?" General Dennings gestures toward the heavy case on the dolly.

"Thank you, General. Davies, you can lead the team to take the payload down to the insertion team below," Dr. Turner instructs, nodding to Davies.

Davies quickly approaches the two soldiers handling the metallic box and guides them out of the room. "The team and I have worked hard to ensure this demonstration will be worth your time. Seeing is believing, after all."

Dr. Turner slowly gestures to the observation window, and General Dennings moves to the glass to look down into the depths of the experimentation chamber, deep within the mountain cavern below.

"Li, could you please start the pre-initiation checklist?" Turner asks. Li Meng begins typing at her terminal. As she works, half of the large observation window lights up with a mirrored projection of her desktop. Charts, graphs, and vector animations fill the glass surface. A pop-up window also displays a feed from the control room camera located in the room below.

The control room is filled with banks of switchboards, server arrays, computer terminals, and other high-tech equipment, all illuminated by flickering LEDs as they process data. Two technicians, clad in white clean-room suits designed to prevent hair, dust, and other contaminants from entering the space, operate the controls. Beyond the common work area in the spacious chamber, a large coiled structure rests on a steel track, elevated about six feet off the floor. The camera zooms to the back of the room, where an elevator door embedded in the granite wall opens smoothly. Davies steps out of the elevator, leading two soldiers who are pushing a cart through a small, clear plastic tunnel that connects the elevator to a large plastic tent. Clean-room suits hang on the wall of the tent. Davies grabs a suit and begins putting it on over his clothes, while the soldiers wait for him to finish.

"What do we expect to see differently this time, Doctor?" Dennings inquires as they patiently observe from above.

"Well, let's not overlook our previous efforts. We achieved excellent results despite the shortcomings of the power source. As I mentioned in my initial briefing to the Consortium, destabilized Element 115 simply cannot maintain the power cycle. Now, with the collider reconfigured and calibrated to harness a sustained cold fusion power loop with minimal fluctuations, the stabilized variant should do exactly what its namesake implies - stabilize the power flow between windows, neutralizing variance, and eliminating the chance of an outage. This will also allow us to push the generator to an output level that can create a significantly larger displacement field during operation. In theory, if the power source holds, the size and distance of the field's reach will be virtually limitless."

"In layman's terms?" the General asks. Doctor Turner grins and removes his glasses to wipe them.

"Sorry, old habits die hard. Basically, we were trying to power an entire city block with the energy generated by a hamster running on a wheel. That's why the fields were so small and only lasted for a short time. Based on our previous results and current projections, by using the stabilized Element 115 now, we should be able to establish long-term temporal displacement rifts, or portals, that will allow you to move large volumes of..." Dr. Turner pauses, noticing the General's stern gaze. "My apologies - I'm doing it again. General, to put it simply, if this works, you'll be able to transport as many soldiers, tanks, aircraft, and whatever else you need through portals we can place anywhere across the globe...and beyond." The General raises an eyebrow, acknowledging his understanding of the concept. The two men turn to gaze silently into the cavern through the glass partition, each seemingly contemplating the implications of this revelation, likely arriving at very different conclusions.

Security Camera - Temporal Loop Generator SubStation

Davies is now dressed in a protective jumpsuit with a hood and clear plastic face shield. With a woosh of decompressed air, he exits the airlock connecting the elevator tunnel. The two Special Forces escorts remain in this transitional area between the elevator and the main substation control room. This space resembles a highly monitored "clean room" environment. As Davies struggles to maneuver the heavy dolly and payload into the main area, two other technicians in personal protective gear quietly work at a bank of control consoles, adjusting dials and switches while monitoring computer screens. At the center of the room stands a thick, rectangular stainless steel structure, about four feet tall and three feet wide. A heavy glass hinged hatch embedded in its smooth surface serves as a windowed port on its face, from which a subtle glow emanates.

Davies slowly steers the heavy roller cart to the center of the room and opens the sealed door atop the metallic crate's lid. A thin mist escapes, revealing residual gas from some type of coolant. Stepping aside, Davies watches as two technicians work together. One technician, wearing thick gloves, uses large locking forceps, while the other operates a console connected to the steel housing.

The technician with the forceps leans down, manipulating them to tighten and pinch something inside the crate. He secures the clamp, locking the tongs in place, and then struggles to gain leverage on the unseen item. After a moment of effort, he lifts a small, black sphere - a pearl of matter - pinched between the forceps. The sphere is so tiny that it would be nearly imperceptible on camera footage, were it not for the Junior Arbiters digitally zooming in. The technician's struggle to lift such a small object is almost comical, resembling a mime pretending to carry something both invisible and impossibly heavy.

Noticing the technician's difficulty, Davies steps in to help, assisting in hoisting the forceps into position over the windowed opening of the thick steel receptacle. Meanwhile, the other technician at the console inputs a series of commands. The electronic locks securing the windowed hatch atop the monolithic structure rotate, and pneumatic doors swing open.

Davies and the technician carefully place the black sphere into the chamber of the housing, then hold steady as they gently unlock and pry open the forceps handles. Both technicians immediately express relief as they remove the forceps. The technician quickly closes the hatch, and the electronic locks engage, rotating back into place. A red light turns green above the small door, and a vacuum seal can be heard pressurizing, ensuring complete closure.

Stepping up to the console, Davies presses the intercom button. His slightly winded voice crackles through to the control room. "We're a go here, Dr. Turner. Requesting permission to initiate the preliminary activation sequence protocols."

Dr. Turner's voice replies over the intercom, "Yes, Davies, proceed. Li, once we have a sample, let me know how everything looks."

Security Camera - Temporal Lab, Observation and Control Room

Li Meng studies the data projections on the large window, her attention focused as new graphics suddenly emerge, spiking and fluctuating alongside a real-time view of the small black ball contained within the illuminated recess of the fixture below. The room waits in silence, all eyes on her, anticipating her response.

"The central core is verified as free of all atmospheric contaminants. The Element 115 is secured and stable on the pedestal, with no deviations. The electron microscope probe indicates that the potential yield of the payload is significantly beyond expectations."

Dr. Turner nods at Li Meng. "Alright, activate the reactor and prepare for acceleration. Gradually increase the power as we modeled. Once the power flow is established, hold at fifteen-percent intervals for evaluation."

"Yes, Doctor," Li responds, beginning to type at her terminal. A subtle yet distinct low hum begins to resonate throughout the building. The windowed display shows graphs and readouts alongside a video feed from the reactor room below, where the small black sphere of Element 115 remains stationary on a metallic concave pedestal in the center of the chamber. "The accelerator is calibrated and ready for the initial pulse," Li announces, awaiting Dr. Turner's command.

"Let's kick the tires and light the fire already, shall we?" Darby interjects obnoxiously. The room collectively ignores his exaggerated enthusiasm.

After a moment of silent contemplation, Dr. Turner turns from the window and looks directly at Li. "Activate," he orders.

Li presses a button on her terminal, and a thin golden beam of laser light emits from the recess of the steel chamber. The concentrated yellow beam strikes the center of the black ball of Element 115. For a brief moment, only a pinprick of white light appears on the surface of the black sphere. Then, the beam penetrates and ignites something within the core of the ebony sphere, causing it to glow a soft fluorescent yellow. The golden light steadily intensifies, radiating outward.

"Internal muons appear to be successfully catalyzing. No ion shed, no unintended expansion. We have achieved cold fusion conversion, Doctor. The reaction is holding at a fifteen-percent threshold output based on commensurate charge," Li reports calmly, though a hint of excitement tinges her voice.

"As we expected. Increase to thirty," Dr. Turner instructs. Li inputs more commands and the intensity of the golden light in the chamber escalates. The camera feed from the reactor below adjusts its exposure, darkening to the point where only the beam's point of impact on the sphere and its immediate glow remain visible. It then shifts to a thermal view, zooming in precisely on where the particle beam strikes the orb. The surface of the black ball appears to morph and flow, as if it were liquefying while still maintaining its perfect spherical shape. Now fluid in its constitution, the glowing orb resembles images of the sun captured by NASA's Solar Orbiter.

"Holding at thirty," Li announces, gazing at her terminal.

General Dennings looks intrigued, even pleased. He steps back to examine the video feed projected on the glass wall of the fusion reaction in greater detail. Darby seizes the moment to lean in beside him, both transfixed by the swirling energy. "I told you it would be worth the wait."

"We'll see," Dennings replies coolly, continuing to watch the feed.

Dr. Turner quickly scans the large display of data before him. Without diverting his gaze from the charts and graphs, he asks, "Li, verify: are you showing any electron shed? Any runoff at all?"

"No, Doctor. Zero," Li responds, cool and steady.

"Phenomenal. Increase the power to seventy percent and instruct Davies and the team below to prepare rift gate X for activation."

"Seventy?" Li asks, surprised.

"Yes, just do it. You were right; the models are solid. If it hasn't decomposed by now, it's not going to," Dr. Turner replies impatiently.

"Seventy percent," Li confirms as she initiates the command via her terminal, then activates the microphone embedded in her console. "Davies, prepare gate X for activation. Clear the floor and stand by for the initiation sequence."

"Uh… Copy that. Clearing the ground team. Preparing gate X," Davies responds.

On the video feed, Davies can be seen directing two technicians in protective gear to the airlock. He then rushes to a nearby console, pulling a thick carabiner clip attached to a retractable metal cord tethered to the steel underside of the console. He hooks it onto a reinforced loop on his jumpsuit belt, flips a series of switches on the terminal's surface, and looks up at the high ceiling of the cavern where a suspended track of rails hangs. Slowly, two identical metallic structures move into place along the rails and descend from above on high-tension steel cables wrapped in electrical rigging. The structures lower in parallel, each consisting of two large polished metal crescents that connect tip-to-tip to form a complete circle. Measuring roughly eight feet in circumference, the circles stop gently, hovering just inches above the floor.

Davies clicks the microphone on his console. "Gates X and Y are in position. Energizing Gate X on your go."

Dr. Turner studies the charts and readouts on the screen, then waves an acknowledgment to Li over his shoulder. "Initiate X."

Li responds through her mic, "You are clear to energize Gate X."

"Roger that. Activating," Davies replies as he lowers a tinted face shield over his clear plastic visor and thumbs a switch on the console in front of him.

The yellow glow within Element 115 intensifies to a blinding white as a brilliant blue light ignites at the center of one of the suspended crescents, presumably known as Gate X. In the observation room above, General Dennings and Darby turn their gazes, startled by the sudden burst of light.

"Apologies, gentlemen. I should have warned you. It fades once the secondary gate is activated. Li, let's exit through the gift shop. Initialize Gate Y," Dr. Turner says.

"Activate Y, Davies," Li commands through the communication channel.

Employee BodyCam: Davies - Temporal Loop Generator SubStation

"Copy that. Activating Gate Y," Davies replies, adjusting a series of controls on the terminal before dramatically pressing a button. Moments later, another flash of blue washes over the room, fading to a flicker as arcs of electricity dance around the silvery frames of each suspended crescent gate. The sporadic surges of energy are the only indication that these portals are actively powered and suspended within the metallic structures. Without this indication, the gates might as well be two polished mirrors reflecting the control room from slightly different angles.

"We appear to have a stable gate, Doc," Davies says enthusiastically as he cautiously moves away from the console, tugging on his lanyard to ensure he is securely tethered. As he steps in front of Gate X, a mirror image of himself appears in Gate Y. "Trippy," he murmurs, awestruck by the newly generated portals before him.

"Pass the benign matter through, Davies," Dr. Turner instructs over the communication channel.

Davies pulls a red rubber ball from his clean-room jumpsuit and raises it for the cameras, as if to announce, "And now, for my next trick." He takes aim and bounces the ball toward Gate X, while a mirror image of his action occurs at Gate Y. After the ball passes through Gate X, Davies awkwardly scrambles a few feet to his right to get into position, hampered by his clean-room attire. Meanwhile, his reflection at Gate Y appears to bounce the ball back to him and also rushes to the adjacent Gate X, crossing the field of view of each portal. As expected, the red rubber ball bounces through Gate Y and returns to Davies' hand. He triumphantly holds the ball up for the audience above and the cameras, letting out a small cheer. "Yes! Doc, we have pass-thru! No visible decomposition."

20:44:10 - Security Camera - Temporal Lab, Observation and Control Room

"Contain yourself, Davies. We're just getting started," Doctor Turner says mildly over the radio. Davies straightens, regaining his composure. "Li, how are we looking?"

She focuses intently on her screen, noticing something. "Minor fluctuation... but I believe it's the field attenuator compensating. We're stable on all nodes, Dr. Turner," Li replies, attentive to her terminal's readouts and data.

Dr. Turner considers this for a moment. General Dennings turns to him, nodding in approval of the demonstration below. "Impressive," he remarks. "Now, what about..."

"Organic matter?" Doctor Turner interjects, pulled from his thoughts about Li's readings. The General nods. "Of course, I assumed you would want to see that we are capable on that front as well. It's a final requirement of the DoD order, after all. We have something prepared for you. Davies, let's push for organic transfer. Show the General what the future of troop transport looks like," Turner says confidently.

"Going live, copy that," Davies responds through his terminal microphone.

Moments later, the two-man crew of lab technicians enters the space, pushing a biomechatronically altered gelada baboon on a gurney. The animal is clearly sedated, showing no signs of struggle against the bindings strapped around its arms, torso, and mechanical legs, which secure it to the wheeled stretcher. Groggy, the baboon scans the room from behind its VR visor, attempting to take in its surroundings.

"We're set here," Davies says over the comms.

"Li, push to ninety-five percent. Mitigate any further possibility of power flux," Dr. Turner instructs without turning around.

Li examines her readouts, biting her lip and wringing her hands as she interprets the data. "I think we can hold it at the current power output levels."

"No, let's go to ninety-five," Dr. Turner insists.

"Ninety-five," Li replies, her voice tinged with hesitation.

"Davies, begin push," Turner says into the mic.

Security Camera - Temporal Loop Generator SubStation

Davies inputs a series of commands, and the two portals lower to floor level, settling a few inches into a shallow recess carved into the ground to accommodate the gates. The lab technicians maneuver the gurney into position with Gate X, rolling it forward under Davies' supervision. The gelada baboon stirs slightly.

DL Primate - VISOR 0060 - POV / HUD

From the gelada's perspective, the video feed captures the gurney being steadily pushed toward and through Gate X. The robotic alloy legs move slightly against their straps, but what stands out is the way the primate's thick, coarse hairs are beginning to stand upright along its torso, a result of the electrostatic charge generated by the portals as it approaches. Agitated and disturbed from a comfortable, sedated slumber, the ape emits a series of laborious, stunted grunts from deep within its chest. The technicians, however, pay no attention and continue to advance the gurney.

As the gurney breaches Gate X's generated portal plane and the primate's metallic prosthetics enter the transfer window, it suddenly reemerges through Gate Y's exit. The beast lets out a much louder and more startled cry. The technicians momentarily pause, instinctively looking up to the control room, awaiting an order. The tiny blue-white arcs of energy dancing around the edges of each gate spasm slightly before stabilizing.

"Proceed," Dr. Turner's voice resonates through the room's intercom. The technicians comply, resuming their steady push forward. The baboon's protests continue and intensify, but the technicians methodically advance the gurney.

* * *

Security Camera - Temporal Lab, Observation and Control Room

"Is that normal?" General Dennings asks, grimacing at the scene unfolding below.

Before Dr. Turner can respond, Darby interjects, "Oh yeah, it's a decommissioned specimen for this reason. Bad temperament. Real troublemaker. We use unsuitable ones as test subjects after they're taken out of rotation, that's all."

"Li, how's the composition girder holding?" Dr. Turner inquires.

"Cellular analysis on the specimen is holding steady between gates," she replies, preoccupied and typing rapidly at her keyboard while glancing quickly between monitors. "But, Doctor... we are detecting a slight fluctuation between the gates, and there's an unusual... anomaly in the power - "

"Very good," Dr. Turner interrupts. "As long as it's holding, let's finish the transfer." He says this impatiently while peering down at the ongoing process below.

Employee BodyCam: Davies - Temporal Loop Generator SubStation

The video tracks Davies as he shadows two technicians who steadily push a baboon through Gate X. The animal screeches more violently in tired protest the further it is pushed. At Gate Y, the wriggling, irritable body of the beast emerges. The technicians maneuver the gurney with two elongated steel rods, careful not to place their hands or arms into the gate's portal field. The baboon's neck, chin, and lower jaw pass through. Suddenly, a flash of blue electric light ripples across the surface of Gate X. The baboon's body suddenly convulses, shaking the entire gurney and causing it to jump and clatter back a few inches on the stone floor. Flickering electric blue light dances along the edges of each gate's frame, thickening into broad, crackling bands of energy. The baboon's lower jaw in Gate Y cries out in anguished croaks, startling the technicians, who lurch to push the final length of the gurney through with their rods. At that moment, in another stunning flash of light, Gate Y shimmers, warbles one last time, and then dissipates entirely, as if the power had been cut. The primate's body immediately ceases convulsing. Davies rushes to the gurney, and the reason for his alarm is clear: the upper half of the primate's skull is missing. Only a steaming, cauterized blister remains, covering the area where the top of its head was previously attached, just above its smoking nostrils. The part of the skull that held the VR helmet is nowhere to be found.

"Doc! Are you seeing this? Holy shit, what happ - " Davies begins before Dr. Turner mutes his microphone.

Security Camera - Temporal Lab, Observation and Control Room

"God damn it all..." Dr. Turner exclaims, a mix of disgust and disappointment in his voice. "Li!"

General Dennings and Darby, both too shocked to speak, turn to Li at the back of the room, who is already taking action. She quickly taps at the console keyboard, generating a series of charts and readouts on the glass wall in front of Dr. Turner for his review. One graph in particular displays a stable line with minor fluctuations over time, followed by a drastic spike that holds its peak before suddenly dropping to zero.

"An anomalous fluctuation followed by an abrupt loss of power. It happened in an instant, Doctor. The cause is unknown, but... there was no way we could have prevented it in that brief window," Li explains. Dr. Turner rubs his temples, trying to digest the data before him. "Pulling up replay for analysis and generating deep scans for review. Standby," Li adds, her voice trembling slightly under stress. A video playback of the catastrophic moment begins on the screen. The baboon's head enters, and the field shimmers.

"No, we don't need fucking playback! This isn't SportsCenter; we all saw what happened!" Dr. Turner exclaims. Startled, Li hits the pause button, freezing the video at the moment when the baboon was passing through the teleportation gate - just before everything went sideways. Dr. Turner sags, averting his eyes from the grotesque image of the contorted primate's last moments. General Dennings shakes his head and begins to walk slowly toward the exit. Sensing his departure, Darby steps into his path and holds up his hands to stop the imposing figure. Dennings halts but shoots him a glare. "Save your nonsense, Darby. We came to see results. This program clearly isn't ready, and it isn't for us."

Darby sputters as Dennings presses on, moving him aside with a broad stroke of his quintessentially militaristic "knife-hand." But like the weasel he is, Darby pivots and quickly positions himself back in front of the door, holding his hands up pleadingly. "Hey now! What do you call that if not results?" he says, pointing to the big screen. "Sure, we lost a little off the top, but ninety percent of that monkey made it through! That's got to count for something!" Darby adds, flustered.

The General appears poised to flatline Darby at that moment, and one can't help but wonder if he would have done so if not for the psychedelic flash of multicolored lights and the strobing from the windowed screen behind him, which drew everyone's attention back to the front of the room. A new video feed is now playing on the floor-to-ceiling glass. Initially, it resembles a chaotic array of flashing blocks and color fragments, possibly digital distortion or some form of dissonant signal processing. Then, the distortion clears, and the feed stabilizes with a clearer image.

"Doctor! We have signal reconnected," Li announces.

An alien landscape fills the screen. Windswept, craggy black rock peaks and precipices tear at the skyline, contrasting sharply against a slate gray sky. Bursts of white lightning roll almost continuously across a desolate valley of dusty, cracked earth stretching into the distance. At first, something large, shapeless, and dark moves across the seemingly abandoned vista. It isn't just moving; it's crawling and writhing, creeping along the horizon in an unusual and unsettling manner. The only sound filtering through the feed is the low hum of the wind whipping across the terrain, a constant static gray noise. Silence fills the room as everyone strains to comprehend the scene unfolding on the screen. Their confusion is heightened by an unusual detail: a digital stamp in the upper right corner of the feed indicates the source of the transmission, ticking seconds away: *"DL Primate - VISOR 0060 - POV/HUD."*

After a moment of silence, Dr. Turner turns to Li. Calm and genuinely curious, he asks, "Li...what in the hell are we looking at?" Li appears both bewildered and fascinated. Without tearing her eyes away from the video transmission, she enters a few keystrokes at her terminal and waits for confirmation with rapt attention. New data flashes on her screen.

"It's real-time. Verified," she says, disbelieving her own conclusion.

"But where... and how..." Dr. Turner mutters just before it happens. The entire video image spins wildly, as if kicked by an unseen force off-camera. In the dizzying motion, a silhouette emerges - large, dark, and contorted - visible between the revolutions of the spinning camera. Then, for just a few seconds, the feed stabilizes. The wind howls, sweeping dust across the alien, barren landscape. Suddenly, the camera begins to lift off the cracked floor, accompanied by a distorted squelching and crunching sound, before the transmission terminates, leaving only a frozen frame of glitchy data and blocky fragments fluctuating on the screen.

"What the hell are we looking at, Turner?" General Dennings demands, with Darby quickly echoing the question. Before Dr. Turner can respond, the room fills with piercing klaxon alarms. The video feed on the large glass window automatically switches to display the alert, presenting visual graphs, charts, and cascading data readouts. Davies' voice, nervous and trembling, comes over the intercom. "Doc! You guys aren't preparing to engage the collider again, are you?" Dr. Turner snaps his head back to Li, who is feverishly inputting commands at her terminal, clearly frustrated.

"Li, what is going on?" Dr. Turner asks. Li doesn't respond, too absorbed in her screens to hear him. Growing impatient, Dr. Turner storms over to her console to see for himself what she is dealing with. "Li! What's the status?!" Li finally looks up from her work, fear and panic etched on her face.

"The reactor is engaged and overclocked. It's set to discharge at a two-hundred percent threshold and... and..." she stutters.

"Two hundred?! Why would... What, Li?!" Dr. Turner shakes her by the shoulders. "Just shut it down."

"I... I can't stop it. We don't have control," Li replies. Darby throws his hands up in disbelief and laughs.

"What? Bullshit. This facility is a closed loop. No external access; all networks are self-contained," Darby exclaims.

Dr. Turner hurriedly checks the terminal readouts, enters his commands, and tries to override the orders. He repeatedly mashes the return button, but his code yields no results. Pressing the microphone on the terminal, he coldly and authoritatively commands, "Davies. Get everyone out of there. Right now." Turning to General Dennings, he grimly states, "We have lost control. Something is at the helm, actively altering the accelerator initiatives, rewriting the code, overclocking the PCs running the algorithms, and queuing up another discharge that could completely overdrive the reactor."

Darby scoffs and steps closer to inspect the screen for himself. "No fucking way. This place can't be hacked," he exclaims.

Dr. Turner shakes his head and glares at Darby. "What exactly does that mean, Turner?" Dennings interjects, cutting to the chase.

Dr. Turner removes his glasses and locks eyes with the General. "I don't know, but we're about to find out." He nods toward the observation windows at the front, where a countdown clock is reflected on the screen. The title reads, "Gate Activation," and the digits count down: 5, 4, 3, 2, 1...

The familiar hum of the reactor intensifies, rumbling through the building. The lights dim slightly as General Dennings, Darby, and Dr. Turner walk slowly to the window. "This isn't a hack," Dr. Turner states as the portal gates in the cavern below begin to power cycle. Blue arcs of crackling light shimmer and ripple around Gates X and Y. The laboratory camera feeds appear on the windows, showing the gates glowing with energy. Their metallic crescents vibrate and rattle, creating an unsettling atmosphere. Suddenly, something wet, red, and shiny is expelled from Gate X, as if hurled from the other side. It clangs to the floor with a dull thud and slides to the center of the lab, leaving a trail of viscous crimson behind it. Dr. Turner grabs a joystick on a nearby console, zooming in the laboratory camera on the object: the crumpled primate VR visor, still affixed to what remains of the top half of the gelada baboon's now bisected skull. With a sound like rending steel, the entire lab quakes as a massive rumbling erupts. The grinding and quaking seem to resonate from the depths of the mountain, causing both portal gates to swing like pendulums from their suspension cables.

21:37:12 09/02/22
Security Camera - Exterior - West Entrance Point Delta / Helipad

The jagged horizon, marked by distant mountain peaks, cuts across the desert sky, crackling with electricity. Rolling thunder echoes as blue orbs of plasma, resembling the fabled ball lightning, materialize just above the concrete helipad. They glide silently across the landing zone, reaching the edge of the pad before floating untethered into the sky. The camera begins to glitch as these electric globules appear in increasing waves around the helipad, each following a magnetic path toward a point beyond the horizon.

Security Camera - Temporal Lab, Observation and Control Room

Davies and his entourage of commandos enter the observation area, visibly anxious. General Dennings turns to his men and swiftly orders them to pack their gear. "Our visit is over. Doctor. Maybe next time."

As he dismisses Dr. Turner and his efforts, Darby raises his hands in frustration and glares at the doctor. With a determined stride, General Dennings heads for the doorway, clearly focused on one mission: to exit the building. Darby scurries to keep up, trailing just behind the General's escort as they approach the door. Suddenly, the lights flicker and go out. The cables suspending the gates snap, recoiling and crashing to the cave floor with a metallic clatter. Remarkably, the gates themselves remain suspended, hovering in midair. Defying gravity, the laws governing their operation seem to be broken, as the rippling energy portals continue to undulate across their surfaces, despite the severed power and coolant cables. Plumes of liquid nitrogen gas from the broken suspension lines billow out, filling the cavern and obscuring the camera's view.

The playback freezes, advancing one frame at a time. The flickering light emanating from each gate creates a strobe effect as it refracts through the foggy gas. One frame is nearly whited out, and in the next, something large and dark appears to emerge from Gate Y. As the frames progress, it becomes clear that it is indeed moving. Long and hinged at joints, eight-foot-long sections of sharply pointed appendages, reminiscent of spider legs, tap and extend to graze the rim of the gate. Seconds pass on the screen before these appendages reach further into the room, gently touching down and exploring the floor space. Something otherworldly is clawing its way through Gate Y. The playback resumes its speed, and a flood of flashing lights and indescribable, otherworldly sounds fills the air as silhouettes that resemble humanoid forms - yet are distinctly not - claw, pull, and lunge forth from each gate. A tangle of limbs, distorted and grotesque forms meld and flow as they tear and grapple with one another, obscured by the white fog of HALON gas and the pulsing emergency strobe lights throughout the large room. Moving with incredible speed, the apparitions vanish in an instant, accompanied by a cacophony of screeches, wails, snarls, and gnashing teeth.

21:39:15 09/02/22
Security Camera - Temporal Lab, Observation and Control Room

"Holy fuck!" exclaims Davies. Everyone in the room freezes, taking stock of the unfolding scene on the security camera feed. General Dennings stares, slack-jawed. The mercenary security detail instinctively raises their rifles, scanning the room for threats while flanking the General in defensive positions. They begin to move in unison across the floor, shepherding the General toward the exit door. Davies and Darby stand dumbstruck, staring up at the screen together.

Dr. Turner whips his head back to Li Meng, shock and disbelief etched across his face as he stammers, "Li! Wh-wha-what is this?!" His voice wavers uncontrollably.

In this moment captured on camera, the playback slows and freezes once again. In the still frame, Li is hunched over the keyboard, tapping away on the console in front of her. Then, as the timecode advances by a single frame, a blurred outline of an oddly shaped figure appears directly behind her. Initially, like digital distortion - a corrupt image that can occur during video transcoding or when certain codecs produce visual artifacts due to encoding errors. However, as the frame advances, it becomes clear that this is not a broken frame. Instead, it reveals a silhouette, or more accurately, a mirage within a silhouette that absorbs the surrounding light at the edges of its form. It's faint but unmistakably present.

In the next frame, the outline of the apparition shifts slightly, yet it retains its stature. It appears somewhat humanoid in shape and relative size, but its proportions and appendages are unsettlingly unnatural. With long, dragging arms resembling tentacles rather than human limbs, an elongated torso, and an oddly shaped oblong head, the figure looms over Li. In the following frame, it extends one long, gangly appendage as if reaching out to tap Li on the shoulder. But in the very next frame, it vanishes altogether, and the tape resumes normal playback speed.

At this moment, with her back turned to Dr. Turner and the other occupants of the room, Li Meng slumps slightly, her shoulders relaxing and her chin tilting down. Although likely imperceptible to most, this gesture is accentuated by the digital zoom focusing on Li, highlighting an aspect of interest noted by the Junior Arbiters during their initial review. It's a good catch. Another moment passes with no movement at all. The image shifts back to full frame as Dr. Turner stumbles across the room, exasperated and clearly agitated by Li's lack of response.

"Li! What the hell is happening in the reactor room down below?" Li slowly turns around, lifting her chin. The camera zooms in on her face as Dr. Turner approaches. Her eyes snap open, revealing two deep, soulless crimson orbs, as if every vessel in her eyes had ruptured, filling them with blood. Dr. Turner halts in his tracks, horrified. "Li! What - what's wrong with you?!" is all he can manage to exclaim.

In a shocking display of speed and agility, Li raises her hand, grasping Dr. Turner by the throat and crushing his windpipe, silencing his panicked voice into a ragged gurgle before snuffing it out completely. Without effort, she lifts him off the ground, nearly twice her mass. The other men in the room freeze in place as Li stares coldly into Dr. Turner's bulging eyes, examining him while he kicks and struggles. Tears of blood stream down her face, a stark contrast to her otherwise uncaring, inhuman expression. Her lack of humanity is underscored as she speaks next.

"WE - ARE - ALL....WE - ARE - DOOM. WE - ARE - HERE." Her voice is booming, guttural, and broken, distinctly not her own. To emphasize her message, she abruptly drops Dr. Turner to the floor in a heap.

THE LAW

PART FOUR

12

A slate of information appears in white text on the computer screen: the rundown and diagnostic data of all sources that comprise the video footage obtained in the field for this linear timeline of events. It reads:

THE LAW - SOURCE CONTENT - VIDEO
- AXON Body Camera: POV Deputy Cove - 4K, 60FPS
- Police Cruiser Samsara MVARS Dash Cam - 1920x1080, 30FPS
- Security Camera, Pappy's Drug Store - 4K, 24FPS
- ATM Camera, Main Street Union Bank & Trust - 1920x1080, 30FPS

Timecode and location data appear in the upper left corner of the screen, tracking the exact or approximate timeline of when the displayed footage was recorded, as assessed by the Junior Arbiters.

17:11:15 09/02/22
Police Cruiser Dash Cam

The cruiser slowly approaches a four-way stoplight. The street sign, suspended by cables, sways gently in the evening breeze and reads

"Main Street." It might as well say "Main Street, USA," as the area seems to have been designed in the mid-1950s, reminiscent of a Norman Rockwell blueprint. Bathed in the golden glow of the setting sun, the four corners feature a two-story motel, a drug store with a half-lit neon sign reading "Pappy's Drug & Supply," a gas station with an attached mechanic's garage displaying a cracked, weathered hand-painted sign, and a small diner simply labeled "24 hr Diner." In a small town where one business dominates a specific service, clever naming conventions are often overlooked. The street, though seemingly calm, has a few cars and pedestrians moving along. Besides this activity, the town seems not only quiet but on the verge of being completely comatose. The hum of the cruiser's idling engine is interrupted when the CB radio crackles to life, and the voice of a middle-aged female dispatcher fills the air.

"Dusty, come in."

A man clears his throat off-camera, and the sound of someone reaching for the CB precedes a reply from inside the cruiser.

"Go for Deputy Cove."

After a brief pause, static erupts again on the CB. "Yes, Deputy. Your favorite frequent flyer is back at it and has requested you… personally."

"Shit…" is heard off-camera from within the cab.

The dispatcher continues over the radio. "Bill Johanssen is reporting livestock damage at his farm. Chickens. He says, and I quote, that it 'definitely might possibly be wolves'… again."

A sigh escapes from the cruiser, followed by muttering. "God damn it… ain't no wolves. Again with this shit, Bill…" Another sigh is heard before the CB clicks to static, and the man responds, clearly irritated but trying to stay composed. "Copy that. I'll swing by his place again right after I grab lunch. This is the second time this week, and it's only Tuesday, Cheryl."

"Yes, Deputy. I'm aware," the woman on the other end replies flatly.

The man sighs. "I'm ten minutes out. Let Bill know I'm coming… again."

"Enjoy your lunch, Deputy," Cheryl responds.

The traffic light turns green, and the cruiser makes a U-turn in the intersection, heading in the opposite direction.

17:49:55 09/02/22
Police Cruiser Dash Cam

* * *

The cruiser rolls down a dirt farm road lined with a dilapidated wooden fence before turning onto a long gravel path. The crunch of gravel beneath the tires drowns out the sounds inside the cab. As the vehicle crests a small slope, a quaint single-story farmhouse, accompanied by a small barn and livestock pen, comes into view a few hundred yards away. The weathered buildings become clearer as the cruiser accelerates, revealing that aside from needing a fresh coat of paint, they are in decent condition. As the cruiser approaches, an elderly man in his sixties, sporting a grey beard and wearing soiled, worn coveralls, emerges from the farmhouse, cradling a shotgun. He takes a few steps, then leans against a post on the porch, watching stoically as the police cruiser parks in front of him. The sound of the cruiser door opening is audible, and through the windshield, the deputy - a well-built, handsome man in his mid-thirties with a squared jaw - steps into view.

"Bill, how are you doing today, buddy?" the deputy asks. Bill shakes his head in disdain, spits a gob of chew onto the ground, and scowls, as if weighing his response.

Finally, with a slight tremble in his voice, he blurts out, "Sons of bitchin' wolves, Dusty. They wiped out nearly every last one. I've got two hens and a busted-up rooster in half-broke shape. That's it. All that's left..."

The deputy appears unfazed by the man's firearm, indicating a familiarity between them. The only hint of caution comes when the deputy halts his approach as the old man gestures toward the barn, inadvertently wavering the shotgun's muzzle in his direction. The weight of the old man's broken, raspy voice contrasts sharply with the quiet rustling of the wind through the dry cornfields flanking the farmhouse and barn, the stalks gently swaying in the evening light. The deputy moves forward, nodding in sympathetic understanding.

"Is that what the shotgun's for, Bill? Wolves?" the deputy asks.

"You bet your ass," Bill replies earnestly. "They're out there."

"Go ahead and lower that for me, would ya, buddy?" the deputy requests as he steps onto the porch. Bill sheepishly realizes his mistake and lowers the shotgun's muzzle to the ground. "Now... did you actually see a wolf this time?"

"Well... no, but I heard 'em. Clear as day," Bill insists.

The deputy takes a deep breath, removes his sunglasses, and leans against the porch post.

"You know we haven't seen one of those wolves come within ten miles of town for years, Bill. I mean... foxes, maybe, but wolves..." he starts, but Bill interrupts, frustration evident as he walks toward the side of the house, rounding the corner to head straight for the barn.

"Come and see for yourself, Dusty! Damnit all! Look at all these feathers, blood, and beaks! No damn fox did this. Not this time. You tell me what's responsible for this if it ain't wolves!" Bill hobbles around the side of the house and disappears from view.

18:01:15
AXON Body Camera: POV Deputy Cove

From Deputy Cove's perspective, we follow Bill around the side of the small farmhouse. A dilapidated chicken coop stands next to the barn, about twenty yards away. The coop's wooden ramp, meant for the chickens to enter their shelter, is split in two and askew, as if kicked aside. The chicken wire surrounding the base of the shack is bent and ripped outward, suggesting it was violently torn off. True to Bill's word, fresh blood and scattered feathers litter the ground, reminiscent of pillowcases ripped open and flung about, then sprayed generously with red paint.

"Jesus almighty..." Deputy Cove mutters into his body camera mic.

Bill stops and shakes his head at the gruesome scene. "You think I was kiddin?" Bill exclaims.

"Holy hell, Bill... They really did a number..." The body camera slowly pans across the scene before Deputy Cove bends down, capturing what he sees. Amidst the dirt and carnage, he gently brushes aside some blood-spattered feathers, revealing a track mark embedded in the soil. It resembles a large paw print. "If this is a wolf track, it's a big one."

"I'm telling you, Dusty. I heard them. There's more than one, and they've got to go. We need to organize a hunting party and shoot every last one of them."

Deputy Cove's body cam perspective shifts as he stands and faces Bill. "Now, Bill, you know we can't just authorize a hunting party for an endangered species, especially if no one's been harmed. We have to follow the proper - "

"Oh, don't give me that horse shit, Dusty. My livelihood's endangered. I'm endangered. If I had been out here when these sons of bitches were sneakin' in to eat my stock, they could have torn me to shreds. I don't care 'bout no California hippies and their eco-terrorist bullshit. I'll take the fight to them! This is my land, forty years strong!" Bill exclaims and gestures with the shotgun to his barn.

"Alright, calm down, Bill. Don't go getting it all twisted. I'll get you the paperwork to get reimbursed from the state. If a protected species damaged your property, which it seems is the case, we'll document it and sort it out with the conservation department. Don't blow a gasket," Deputy Cove says.

Bill takes a moment to let his anger subside. From Deputy Cove's body cam, we see a closer view of the coop, revealing scratches along the woodwork - possibly claw marks.

In the background, Bill shuffles around, muttering to himself. "Ever since that company came an' set up shop on the mountain, I swear these damn wolves got pushed back this way. Them and the earthquakes, I am telling you, those people are probably digging in that mountain, poisoning the damn water table, causin' earthquakes or something, and it's driving the damned wolves back this way. They should be paying me reparations…"

Deputy Cove sighs as he inspects the chicken coop's twisted wire and splintered wood base, half-listening to Bill's ramblings.

"Yeah, I hear you, Bill. Earthquakes and wolves… Alright, I'll write it all up and get the paperwork submitted." Deputy Cove stands and approaches Bill, who gazes at the horizon, squinting toward a flashing beacon on the mountain in the waning afternoon sun. "I've got what I need. Listen, maybe you should stay inside after dark for a few days. If it really is the wolves from the release program, they'll be in a pack. You don't want to get caught off guard," Deputy Cove advises, genuine concern in his voice for the old-timer.

Bill shrugs, pats his shotgun, and spits a brown splatter. "No chance in hell they're getting the drop on me, Dusty."

13

The deputy's cruiser leaves Bill's farm, quickly picking up speed. The CB clicks on, and Deputy Cove speaks into the mic. "Cheryl, I'm 10-19 from Bill's farm, headed back to the station to fill out some paperwork and grab some ibuprofen."

A moment of silence passes before static crackles. "Copy that, Dusty. I'm putting a fresh pot on. It'll be ready when you get here," Cheryl replies.

"Yeah...coffee sounds good. Thanks." The CB clicks off.

The cruiser continues down the desolate, dark two-lane highway for another fifteen to twenty seconds. In the distance, a pair of flashing green and red lights emerges on the horizon. Initially faint, they quickly grow larger and brighter - anti-collision aircraft lights. Moments later, the low, distinct thumping of rotor blades slicing through the air joins the silhouette of a Blackhawk helicopter as it flies overhead, heading straight for the mountain range in the distance. The cruiser maintains its speed, undeterred.

* * *

19:47:43
AXON Body Camera: POV Deputy Cove

From Deputy Cove's perspective, the inside of Pappy's Drug Store comes into view as he waits to complete his transaction at the checkout counter. A teenage clerk hands him his change, and Deputy Cove picks up a bottle of Dr. Pepper and a small travel tube of ibuprofen from the counter.

"Thanks, Randy. Have a good night, man," he says to the young clerk. Randy, the boy behind the counter, waves goodbye with a smile. It's a small town where everyone knows each other, and politeness is the norm. Deputy Cove steps outside onto the sidewalk, pops open his soda, and cracks the vial of ibuprofen, quickly swallowing a few pills with a sip of his drink. Night has fallen rapidly over the town. The streetlights are illuminated, and a few neon signs flicker to life in the corner store windows and shopfronts. Quiet. There is a reason that small towns are synonymous with quiet. As a matter of fact, the only sound disturbing the otherwise perfectly serene night is light shuffling and some garbled muttering from nearby. Deputy Cove turns, and the perspective shift reveals a disheveled man stumbling along the sidewalk near the police cruiser, clutching a bottle wrapped in a brown paper bag.

"Jim. Hey, whoa, easy there," Deputy Cove says as he quickly moves to catch the old man, stabilizing him before he can topple headfirst into a trash can teetering near the curb.

The old drunk, Jim, looks up and grins, revealing half of his teeth, slurring and spitting as he greets the deputy. "Heya, Dusty! Look at you. So big now! I remember when you were just a kid…"

Deputy Cove steps back, recoiling from the drunkard's strong breath. "Whoa, Jim, you're really deep in the barrel today, aren't you? How much have you had to drink?"

The old man shakes his head, shrugging incredulously. "I haven't - didn't have a drop. Sober as a nun," he says, chuckling to himself and nearly collapsing. Again, Dusty catches the old drunk before gravity claims him and hoists him upright.

"Jeez, Jim…come on. Let's get you to the station. You know I can't leave you out here. You're going to get hit by a car…"

The old man hiccups and obediently tumbles headfirst into the backseat of Deputy Cove's cruiser. Small-town consequences, small-town routines, small kindnesses.

14

Springerville Police Station Security Cameras - 4K, 60FPS

The well-worn paint near the front door is rubbed bare in spots, exposing the sturdy red brick of the building beneath, particularly where the chairs lining the lobby wall have worn against it over the years. Separated by a long oak countertop with a single waist-high hinged door, the office area contains three desks, each cluttered with knickknacks, personal photos, and stacks of paperwork. The outdated, no-frills utility of the adjacent four small holding cells highlights that the small-town jailhouse was designed for the volume - or lack thereof - of small-town criminals likely to require jailing.

Deputy Cove pours himself a cup of coffee at the back of the room while adjusting a CB radio dial that sputters and crackles with static. On the screen, the text "CHERYL WILKINS" appears over a plump, curvy woman with larger-than-life hair. In her mid-fifties and wearing a sequined sweater, Cheryl sashays through the office, rummaging through her equally grandiose purse. Her hoop earrings sway with each step, and the familiar twang and motherly tone of her voice echo from earlier communications over the police CB. "That radio has been acting up for the last hour, hun. We might need to call in a repair."

"Yeah, sounds like it, Cheryl," Deputy Cove replies, mildly annoyed as he tweaks another dial on the old radio before giving up. He shifts his attention to methodically tearing open a single-serve coffee cream container and pouring it into his coffee.

"Don't forget to check on Jim every so often and make sure he's rolled up properly on his side, Dusty..." Cheryl calls over her shoulder as she moves toward the front door.

"Jim's a seasoned pro, Cheryl; he'll be fine," Deputy Cove responds, half paying attention as he rips open a sugar packet and mixes it into his coffee.

"Yeah, well, no less. If he croaks on property, you're filling out the extra paperwork," she says dryly before scanning the room with a flustered look. "Now, damnit all... have you seen my glasses lying around here?" She looks up at the deputy, exasperated.

Deputy Cove slowly strides over to her, coffee in hand. "You know why I'm the lead investigator around here, don't you?" Deputy Cove asks seriously, sipping his coffee. Cheryl looks at him, confused and a bit annoyed, as he slowly shifts his gaze to the top of her head, then locks his eyes on her. She blushes, reaches up to her big hair, and discovers her glasses perched atop her head.

"Thank you, Deputy. I hope you have a nice, quiet night," she replies.

"Is there any other kind around here?" Deputy Cove grins.

Cheryl waves as she exits through the front door. Deputy Cove approaches a cell and peers in through the bars, rapping his knuckles on the steel. "Hey, Jim, roll over!" he calls out loudly, barely eliciting a drunken grumble from within the cell.

20:30:12

Deputy Cove sits at his desk, typing on the keyboard. He pauses to cross-reference the screen, shuffles a stack of paperwork, and identifies a document, nodding to himself. After entering a few more keystrokes, he leans back in his office chair, groaning as he stretches and yawns. He folds his arms and kicks his feet up on the desk - it's nap time.

20:45:12

Deputy Cove is sound asleep in his office chair. The station is quiet except for the light, sporadic, ragged snoring coming from Jim's cell. Suddenly, the piercing squeal of the CB cuts through the air, startling Deputy Cove awake and prompting a series of throaty snorts from Jim.

Deputy Cove jolts up, adrenaline surging, his hands instinctively grabbing his gun belt before he steadies himself. He glances at the screeching CB and briskly strides over to the radio, snapping the power dial to the OFF position. The squelching persists for a moment despite the power being cut. Frustrated, Deputy Cove flips the switch from ON to OFF repeatedly until the radio finally falls silent. Jim grumbles from his cell, annoyed.

"Yeah, yeah, sorry to bother you, Sleeping Beauty. Go back to bed, will ya?" Deputy Cove grumbles at Jim. "Piece of junk radio... antiquated like everything else here." He groggily heads to the coffee station, engaging in his familiar caffeine and sugar ritual once more.

21:37:55

Deputy Cove hunches over his desk, filling out paperwork yet again. The front door jingles as another uniformed officer, a man in his early thirties, enters the lobby carrying a worn department-issued jacket and a brown paper lunch sack. "CARY DONNER - POLICE OFFICER, SPRINGERVILLE PD" appears in text over the newcomer.

"Hey, Cary," Deputy Cove greets.

"Hey man, how you hanging? Anything shaking tonight?" Cary replies.

Deputy Cove lazily gestures toward the cell at the back of the room. "Well, we've got Springerville's finest sleeping one off in the drunk tank. And a bunch of Bill's chickens got taken out on the farm."

"No kidding... dogs or coyotes this time?" Cary asks, amused as he prepares a cup of coffee.

"Eh, probably coyotes. Not sure, though... they took more than usual. Shitload of feathers..." Deputy Cove says while tidying his desk and grabbing his jacket off the chair, preparing to leave for the night.

"Cool. I'm sure he'll keep us updated. He makes sure we have every bit of intel on those damn cluckers," Cary replies, settling into his own chair.

"Yeah, he really does... he tried to give me the name of each one," Deputy Cove says, lost in thought. "Speaking of being out at Bill's, did you happen to see that helicopter flying low over town this evening? It nearly buzzed me while I was out there."

"A chopper? Nah, I was at Maisy's until I came here. Don't hear much of anything when I'm with her, if you know what I mean," Cary says, grinning widely.

Deputy Cove rolls his eyes. "Yeah, we all get what you mean."

"Bird's probably headed out to the mountain like they do every so often," Cary says, sipping his coffee and rifling through a stack of paperwork.

"Yeah, maybe. This one looked different, though - not a civilian transport. More like a heavy-duty military bird," Deputy Cove says as he shrugs on his jacket and grabs his keys from the desktop. "Well, anyway, I'm out for the night. I've had enough policing for one day in this podunk town." Cove starts across the room toward the door. Just as he reaches the threshold, the overhead lights in the station pulse in a rolling flicker from one end to the other.

21:39:15 09/02/22

Deputy Cove and Cary both notice the change, glancing up at the dusty fluorescent bulbs overhead. A low, almost imperceptible HUM begins to rise and fall, picked up by the camera's microphone, in sync with the brightness of the bulbs growing in intensity and then dimming. Suddenly, the CB radio erupts, screeching at full volume. Cary jumps, bolting upright in his chair. In the back of the room, Jim groans from the prison cell, irritated at being disturbed once again from his drunken slumber.

"Jesus, that thing has been haywire all night!" Cove exclaims, startled and annoyed. Cary stands to move toward the radio. Just before he can reach it, the lights pulse again, dimming to near darkness before blooming back to full brightness. The CB radio screeches in tandem with the lights, as if both were connected to the same faulty electrical circuit. Jim's groaning escalates from a low grumble to an eerie, high-pitched bellow, matching the tone of the radio's squeal. It sounds animalistic and woeful, like a creature caught in a snare, calling out for its pack. The combined noise creates a dissonant, grating symphony.

"Easy, Jim! It's just the damn radio, buddy. Cary, turn that thing off!" Cove snaps.

Cary flips the power switch on the CB, but strangely, the noise persists. In fact, his action seems to have the opposite effect. The volume intensifies, and the pitch of the sound from the speaker rises to an ear-piercing whine. Cary covers his ears, looking dumbfounded back at Cove. Jim's howling continues, but now it emerges deep within him, evolving into a guttural growl. The lights flicker before brightening again to an almost blinding intensity, overwhelming the camera's sensor so that only silhouettes and outlines of the figures and sharp edges in the space are discernible. The whine of electrical current overload crescendos until, suddenly - POP! POP! POP! The fluorescent tube lights overhead shatter, clearly overwhelmed by the surge of power.

"Holy shit!" Cary yells, lowering the brim of his hat to shield his eyes from the falling glass.

The infrared mode on the station's security cameras activates in the darkness, rendering everything in a milky white grayscale. In this moment, the eyes of Deputy Cove and Officer Cary glow white hot. For a brief flash - no more than half a second - a third set of eyes shines from the back corner of Jim's cell.

Deputy Cove stumbles in the dark and yanks the CB from Cary's hands. He raises the unit over his head then slams it down violently onto the ground. The CB disassembles, components and diodes scattering all over the room and floor. Then…silence. No squealing. No flickering lights. No bellowing from Jim.

21:42:05 09/02/22
ATM Camera, Main Street Union Bank & Trust - 1920x1080, 30FPS

A sedan horn honks loudly off-camera before the vehicle careens into view, speeding down Main Street. Bright flashes of blue lightning crackle in the sky overhead as the car's headlights dim and flicker. It veers violently off the road, mounts the curb, and crashes into a telephone pole. The middle-aged woman driving lurches violently into the steering wheel, crumpling in the front seat as the hood concaves. No seat belt. The horn continues to blare. A man in coveralls and a baseball cap emerges from a nearby hardware store and rushes to the vehicle.

As the man opens the door, the driver slumps over and falls onto the pavement, blood streaming down her face from the impact. The man shouts something, but his voice is drowned out by the blaring horn. He frantically waves for another man standing in the hardware store doorway to assist him. Initially unaware of the situation, the second man suddenly sees the woman on the ground beginning to regain consciousness and propping herself up. As she turns, her eyes emit a soft blue glow. Moments later, the first man screams - again inaudible over the horn - as she claws at his leg and groin, pulling him down to the asphalt. In an instant, she is on him, tearing out his throat with her teeth. Blood spills onto the road as the second man approaches, staggering at the horrific sight. A few townsfolk begin to emerge from the corners of the frame: a mother with a child, an elderly woman, and a plump older man wearing a butcher's apron. They all stand in shock as the woman slowly rises, blood dripping from her head and flesh hanging from her teeth.

When the good Samaritan also rises, his eyes glowing with the same pale blue aura, that's when they all flee.

21:44:55 09/02/22
Security Camera, Pappy's Drug Store - 4K, 24FPS

A pharmacist behind the dispensary counter checks labels on prescription bottles against his clipboard inventory sheet. He barely has time to turn around as a body lunges over the counter and tackles him to the floor, scattering orange pill bottles everywhere. A brief and violent struggle behind the counter is visible only through flailing legs and arms. Then, two figures rise: the pharmacist and a blue-collar man, perhaps a ranch hand, both with the same blue eyes.

21:46:07 09/02/22
Springerville Police Station Security Cameras - 4K, 60FPS

The infrared camera mode shuts off in the station, and dim red light from the exit signs and the crimson emergency lights that have activated along the back wall now illuminate the space. Jim lies motionless atop his cot, on the opposite side of the cell from where his eyes, or what appeared to be his eyes, had been just moments before.

Deputy Cove and Cary freeze. After a moment, Cary starts to laugh nervously. "Hol-ee shit, man! I knew the wiring was old in this joint, but hot damn!"

Deputy Cove relaxes his stance and shakes his head. He pulls a flashlight from his belt and clicks it on, scanning the floor. The beam reveals glittering fragments of the radio's internal components and the shards of shattered glass from the overhead fluorescent lights. "Damn. We're gonna need a new radio." The two share a nervous laugh, but their brief moment of relief is abruptly interrupted by a dull, sickening noise: CLaNG-THWACK! CLaNG-THWACK! Metal on flesh…

Deputy Cove directs his flashlight toward the cell, where Jim, the town's harmless drunkard, stands rigidly at attention. In the dim crimson glow of the emergency light, mixed with the penetrating beam of Cove's flashlight, Jim's haggard face is illuminated as he grips the cell bars, blood trickling from a wound on his head. Both men are left speechless, frozen in place. "Jim…" is all Cary manages to say before the frail old man leans back against the bars and then propels himself headfirst into the steel cage once more.

Blood splatters from a fresh gash across his forehead, hitting the concrete floor at the lawmen's feet and creating a thick spray across Cary's boot. Cary startles, stunned into silence. Deputy Cove, however, snaps into action. He rushes to the cell door, fumbling with his keyring.

"Jim! No!" is all he can shout before Jim rams his skull into the bars again with a dull, wet CLANG! THWACK! of flesh and bone against steel. Blood pours from Jim's head wound now, his left eye bulging from the socket, likely due to internal pressure from the trauma. Cove struggles to insert the key into the lock, finally managing to throw the cell door open. He halts as Jim turns his disfigured face toward him.

"Doom. We ArE ALL - DOOM!" Jim growls in a voice that is not his own, lunging at Deputy Cove.

Deputy Cove stumbles backward as he grapples with the old man, losing his balance. Jim snarls, snapping at him in an attempt to bite as Deputy Cove tries to subdue the bloodied, intoxicated figure, wrestling him to the ground. Despite being considerably older and previously drunk, Jim surprisingly matches Deputy Cove's strength and agility, writhing and contorting to escape Cove's grip. Then, with seemingly supernatural strength, he swiftly twists and grabs Deputy Cove by his shirt, lifting him nearly a foot off the ground with ease. Cary stands outside the cell, frozen in place, watching with a slackened, trembling jaw.

Deputy Cove kicks at the elderly man, whose bloodied, wrinkled face is twisted into a grin, revealing gnarled, red-stained teeth and a hideous, bulging blood-red eye. With a voice that seems to rumble from his very core, Jim hisses, "You - are - doomed" as he squeezes Deputy Cove's chest through his uniform. Cove struggles to breathe, wincing in pain.

"Cary! Get - the hell - in - here!" Deputy Cove manages to shout.

Snapping out of his stupor, Cary lunges into the cell, his hand instinctively reaching for the gun holstered at his side. Jim's gaze shifts to Cary, and like a wildcat cornered, he tenses every muscle in his body. With a flick of his wrist, the frail old man tosses Deputy Cove against the back wall of the cell, sending him crumpling to the floor like a puppet with cut strings. Cary draws his pistol, aiming it at Jim. Blood continues to flow from the gash on Jim's head as he crouches low, coiling like a predator ready to pounce, eyes locked on Cary.

"Jim! Freeze right there! Hold it now - right there, you hear?!" Cary stammers.

Deputy Cove mutters, winded, and steadies himself against the cinder-block wall in the corner, struggling to catch his breath. Jim appears oblivious to Cary's instructions. He steps menacingly forward, grinning through clenched teeth at Cary, plodding ahead one ragged step at a time. "DoOm..." he hisses again, his eyes rolling back in his head, one bulging eye trailing the other due to injury. Cary, terrified, glances over at Deputy Cove, who has regained some composure and is now upright against the cinder-block wall near the fixed bench in the cell. "Cove, you alri - "

That momentary glance away was all it took. With Cary's attention diverted from the predator in the cage right before him, a wolf in drunkard's cloth... Jim seizes the instant to strike with frightening and unnatural speed. In that half-second, he bites down, latching onto Cary's throat, then rips and tears the flesh, unleashing a geyser of dark red blood. Jim spits out Cary's jugular, a bit of larynx, and a chunk of surrounding tissue onto the cell floor, grinning a twisted crimson smile. "Animalistic" can't adequately describe the act. While it embodies savagery, blind brute force, and unbridled carnal ferocity, it is also defined by mechanical finesse - motor skills honed through evolutionary necessity to the point of being indistinguishable from instinct. The ruthless efficiency and precision in his actions waste no energy in accomplishing the task. For all the attributes that support survival of the fittest, it fits the bill. But the vehemence, the delight - that is something inhuman and beyond beastly.

Vehemence burns in the eyes of the man, now transformed into a demon, a dark and glinting madness. Coal and fire flicker in those windows where a soul once resided. The fire light is burning in those windows, but Jim is not home; if he is, he is tied to a chair in the attic of his own insanity. Cary collapses to the floor, clutching his throat, blood cascading from the wound. In an instant, the officer loses all blood pressure and crumples in a heap at Jim's feet. Deputy Cove stands ashen and hunched, recoiling at the horror, yet somehow manages to draw his pistol on Jim. Jim turns to him slowly, irreverently, almost coyly. He spits a chunk of Cary's throat onto the floor, hocking it at Deputy Cove's feet.

"YoU'Re...aLL...DeAD. YoU ARE ALL...DoOOOooM," the drunkard rumbles from deep within. He hunches low, as if preparing to lunge.

Deputy Cove's hand trembles as he steadied his service pistol at Jim. "Jim! Stop!"

Jim crouches deeper into his stance when, suddenly, an explosion rocks the building, shaking the camera's view. The entire frame of the security camera tilts as the wall behind the old man erupts in a wave of cinder-block fragments and dust. Jim is obscured in the cloud, and Deputy Cove is sent sprawling to the floor once more. A moment passes before the dust begins to dissipate. Cove rises, stunned, coughing while waving his hands in a futile attempt to clear the air. Jim is nowhere to be seen. In his place lies the steaming, crumpled hood of a wrecked pickup truck, now covered in debris. The driver, a middle-aged woman, is the only other figure visible in the scene. Slumped over the steering wheel, she is bloodied, disheveled, and unconscious. Deputy Cove stands amidst the dust and engine smoke in shock, staring at the gaping hole in the side of the jail.

21:45:13
AXON Body Camera: POV Deputy Cove

From Deputy Cove's perspective, a diffused yellowish-orange glow emanates from the truck's hazard lights, casting a warm light against the smoky, hazy night. As Cove navigates over piles of crumbled rubble and cinderblocks, he peers through the gaping hole in the building's side created by the truck, noticing the flickering light intensifying beyond the wreckage. Staggering forward, he checks the woman's pulse; her head is tilted, eyes wide open - she is unmistakably dead. Cove presses on, stumbling over broken cinderblocks as he pushes past the crumpled truck.

Reaching the tailgate of the destroyed vehicle, which hangs precariously outside the jail, he looks across the street into the darkness. The familiar silhouettes of storefronts and shops are now illuminated by raging fires that lick at the night sky with bright waves of orange flames.

Cove steps to the edge of the sidewalk and into the smoky street. He coughs, suddenly winded. His heavy, short breaths echo loudly over the body camera microphone as the camera pans to the right, revealing chaos along the entire length of the shop fronts. Bathed in firelight, a few townspeople wander aimlessly, while others run and scream for help along the street and sidewalk.

"What... in God's name..." is all Deputy Cove can manage as he turns to look down the street in the opposite direction. He startles and trips as a lifted truck roars past, clips the curb, and careens down the street, plowing over the adjacent sidewalk embankment. The vehicle takes out a stop sign before slamming into a storefront window a few buildings away. The body-cam perspective distorts and shakes as Deputy Cove stumbles, grasping a nearby light pole to steady himself, his knees buckling as he pulls himself up. He is clearly in distress.

The nightmarish version of Small Town USA is underscored by the distant screams and wailing of townsfolk, accompanied by the howling of dogs. A waveform appears on screen, revealing an anomaly in the footage embedded in the audio - something enhanced by the Junior Arbiters who first reviewed it. The waveform decibel meter indicates an increase in gain, making the audio louder and clearer. What follows is a cacophony of anguished wails - not human voices or animalistic shrieks, but something...else. Something otherworldly. A symphony of dissonance and pained vocalizations grows closer and louder as the footage unfolds.

HELL indeed appears to have been unleashed in Springerville.

THE ADVENT

PART FIVE

15

A pop-up window appears on screen. A direct notification from the Junior Arbiters.

REAL-TIME DATA POINT INSERTION NOTIFICATION

I click on the notification and the report populates.

SOURCE: International Space Station – Deep Space Receiver Array
   TRANSMISSION TYPE: Narrowband Radio Signal > Frequency-Shift Keyed (FSK) > Binary Modulation Detected
   ENCODING: Encapsulated Visual Data Blocks – Linguistics Team Transcription in progress
   TRANSMISSION BAND: 1420 MHz (Hydrogen Line – Protected Spectrum)
   SIGNAL STATUS: Repeating. Structurally Redundant. Non-random.
   TRANSMISSION TIME: 21:39:15 UTC

Interesting. The timestamp of the new content is no coincidence. But the origin of the signal? That's what pulled me forward in my seat. A deep space signal? On the hydrogen line?

The hydrogen line - 1420 megahertz - is one of the quietest and most universal frequencies in the electromagnetic spectrum. It's the natural radio emission from neutral hydrogen atoms, the most abundant element in the universe. Because it's so universal - and so quiet - astronomers and physicists have long speculated it would be the cosmic "meeting place" for any species intelligent enough to build a transmitter. You don't stumble across this frequency by accident. You aim for it.

The signal itself was narrowband - razor-thin and focused. Not the kind of noisy broadband static you'd get from a quasar or pulsar. This was deliberate. The payload rode in as frequency-shift keyed bursts - like Morse code on a carrier wave. Each shift between tones corresponded to bits of binary data. And that data, when reconstructed properly, didn't form sound.

It formed pictures.

Then it appeared.

A long, repeating string of code.

Cryptic. Glyphic in nature.

There was something captivating about it…undeniably intentional.

Each frame in the sequence was an encoded 64x64 binary array - ones and zeroes rendered into pixel grids. Static at first glance, but when stitched together in sequence, they formed coherent glyphs. Some sort of visual language. Symbology. Possibly even an evolving syntax based on familiar markers.

The linguistics team believed the structure was intentional - each frame a lesson, each glyph a word, a sentiment…something else?

Somewhere in those blocks was meaning.

And buried deeper than that - perhaps a puzzle piece and a purpose.

The codebreakers had just begun.

SYNCHRONICITY

PART SIX

16

This event was a slow burn but it had gotten intriguing. The Juniors had done a fairly decent job sifting through the preliminary footage and trimming the reels down for my review. Now, the moment we call "convergence" was frozen on my monitor screen, split into a four-pane window, with each quadrant flickering and distorted, showcasing each scene and set of characters in our little small-town horror show in synchronicity according to the timeline.

The Juniors synced up the video feeds based on timestamps and geotags embedded in the footage or other earmarks they identified within the critical incidents. It could be a clock on a wall, the alignment of celestial bodies in the night sky, or someone verbalizing the time on camera. It's not always that we get decent high-quality feeds from so many perspectives that actually sync up to the exact time code, so seeing these four feeds play out with so much overlapping footage was a bit of a treat.

21:39:15

Nine thirty-nine and fifteen seconds, Mountain Standard Time. That was the exact moment of convergence in this unfolding tale for these four seemingly unrelated groups of souls. The instant the dookie hit the proverbial splatter fan, so to speak. This was the moment immediately after those lab coats fired up their big particle collider in the mountains, and things went sideways in this little hole known as Springerville. The Juniors synced and ingested this segment of footage into the playback system, allowing me to view the four divergent perspectives simultaneously or toggle between each feed independently to watch them full-screen as individual clips.

Obviously, it would be too much for untrained observers to try to absorb four independent segments of video playback at once. Any average citizen or casual observer attempting to analyze even two clips simultaneously would find it a laughable exercise, leaving countless critical details overlooked. But hell, I'm a pro. I've honed my skills over the decades and can handle up to eight streams of data without external chemical stimulus. I once managed thirteen for a stretch with the agency-prescribed pep pills, but that can be taxing over long periods, not to mention the lasting implications those little pills can have. You really don't want to rely on that crutch more than once a month or it can become habit-forming. Discipline, time, and natural ability are the only ways to develop this trade, and it didn't happen overnight. It took time and dedication, mind you.

I could let all four screens roll at double speed if I felt crunched for time, and I wouldn't miss a frame of detail. This file hadn't been given code magenta status, though, so there was no need for showboating. Plus, it was starting to get interesting.

When I press PLAY on the master control panel, the distortion on screen clears, and all four panes come into focus. Each quadrant begins to tell its respective aspect of the story in tandem.

17

21:52:11
Police Cruiser Samsara MVARS Dash Cam
TOP-LEFT QUADRANT OF THE SCREEN

A disco of red and blue strobe lights splashes across the street and storefronts, mingling with the steady flickering orange emanating from the burning vehicles and buildings on Main Street. Deputy Cove's police cruiser speeds down the road, weaving around chunks of rubble and debris scattered throughout what was once a tidy, peaceful street. His frantic voice can be heard in the cab of the cruiser as he attempts to raise emergency assistance on the radio.

"This is Deputy Cove of Springerville PD! Come in, Apache County Sheriff's Station! We have a mass casualty event. Come in - anybody!" STATIC and SQUELCHING from the radio are all that reply. "Shit! Come on!" Deputy Cove exclaims.

Just then, the silhouette of a shuffling body cuts through the smoke and haze clouding the street ahead. The cruiser screeches to a stop. "Jesus Christ..." Deputy Cove says in disbelief before unbuckling his seat belt. A moment later, the car door opens, and Cove appears at the edge of the frame near the hood of the cruiser, cautiously approaching with his hand hovering over his holster. He calls out to the person shrouded in haze who is shuffling across the street.

"Cher - Cheryl...is that you?" he asks as the figure's profile becomes a bit clearer, though still obscured by thick haze and now shuffling away from him.

The wafting smoke clears for a brief moment, and indeed it is Cheryl, the matronly receptionist from the police department, moving aimlessly through the chaos and smoke. Deputy Cove's posture relaxes as he steps forward.

"My God, Cheryl, what the hell happened out here? Jim lost his mind back at HQ...he...he attacked Cary. Unbelievable, he lost..."

Cheryl doesn't need to say anything to stop Deputy Cove cold in his tracks. All she has to do is turn toward him, her matted hair clearing her face, and he sees what he needs to know: her eye sockets are hollow and scooped, leaving behind dark red, soulless cavities. Her mouth is agape, dribbling blood from where her tongue had once been, and her ears have been cleanly severed off. Cheryl, once the calming den mother of the police precinct and dispatcher of information, can neither see, hear, nor speak of the evils that have befallen her, her wounds making it virtually impossible to sense the hellscape she now wanders through. She witnessed it firsthand and became a part of the horror itself.

"My God..." is all Cove can utter.

Yet somehow, despite lacking all her sensory appendages, she seems to sense his presence. As she stops and turns her butchered visage toward him. She stumbles and then regains her footing. Her hand reaches into her oversized purse, still hanging at there side limply and she retrieves a small revolver pistol. Cove recoils, nearly falling over the hood of his cruiser as he backpedals.

"No, no, no... Cheryl. Stop. Please, stop..." Cove manages to say. Cheryl does not comply, perhaps unable to hear him at all. Yet somehow, she knows he is there. She aims blindly in his direction and fires a shot over Deputy Coves shoulder, the round ricocheting off a nearby building. Her mouth stretches open wide as the rotund woman unleashes a ragged, bellowing moan from deep within her chest and she lumbers forward, waving the pistol, arms outstretched, grasping and swiping with her free hand at the air where he stood only a moment before. Cove stumbles back over the cruiser, arms outstretched. Cheryl continues to lurch forward, her gargling growing louder as it transforms into a throaty, broken, syllabic rasp from deep within her gut.

"Fe-E-BLe... We-Ak... Be-aST... Bo-D-y..."

Cheryl aims the gun in Cove's direction, wildly scraping at the air with her long, splintered, yellow-painted press-on fingernails with her other hand. The skin on her large arms and legs is scratched and bloodied in patches, but she seems to pay no mind to her own injuries as she hunts blindly for her prey.

Cove unholsters his sidearm and aims with a shaky hand as his colleague closes the gap. As if sensing his presence, Cheryl quickly lunges for him and manages to grab hold of Cove, who responds by grappling with her pistol hand while simultaneously deflecting her wild, claw-like swipe, narrowly avoiding being grazed by her yellow nails. Cove takes advantage of the clinch, securing her wrist and twisting her revolver away from him. Another shot cracks through the air as Cheryl squeezes the trigger and writhes against him, matching his strength. Her butchered face twists, her aggression intensifying. She begins to overwhelm the capable deputy, pressing her ample mass forward while leveraging down, the revolver edging closer to an angle that would mean a certain head shot on Cove. "No! Cheryl, stop!" Cove pleads as he struggles to restrain her hands. Then she squeezes the trigger once more. CLICK. The revolver is empty. Suddenly, Cheryl slumps and goes limp, dropping the pistol and falling directly into Cove's tight embrace as he prevents her from crashing to the asphalt.

Cove seems startled, unsure what to do. Render aid? Restrain her? Then, making the decision for him in a flash, Cheryl lifts her tortured and mangled face, her empty eye sockets fixing on Cove's horrified gaze just inches from his face. "We-AK MaN-NN-N!" Cheryl belches from deep within her chest.

Dark, coagulated blood sprays Deputy Cove's face and uniform lapel as she forces the air out of her lungs in a bubbling blast. He recoils and pulls his hand away from his side to wipe his face. Cheryl seizes the opportunity in that instant. In a swift, jerking motion, the once matronly and slow-moving sentry of the small-town precinct performs a maneuver that would make the most seasoned self-defense practitioner proud as she locks her grasp on his pistol. Lucky for Cove, he is amped with adrenaline, because had he been a microsecond slower and not reacted quickly enough to lock her wrist, he would have lost control of his weapon completely.

Not that it seems to matter much, though.

Through bloodied lips and cracked teeth, Cheryl's smile stretches and twists. She effortlessly begins to leverage the pistol, turning it upward and back around on Deputy Cove as he grunts and struggles to maintain his grasp on it. Cove hollers in pain as his wrist bends. The strain and shock etched on Cove's face is something I have seen so many times before in execution videos and other records where the subject comes face-to-face with imminent death. It is part shock, part disbelief, and a pinch of terrible understanding of what is to come. With that twisted and broken smile frozen on her tortured face, she continues to torque and manipulate the angle of the pistol back on him.

"No! No! Cheryl! It's me! Cove!" the deputy stammers in anguish. Cheryl's unflinching, frozen smile persists, locked on Cove.

Then, with sudden and exacting brute force and no regard for self-injury, she lurches her head back and snaps it forward in a whiplash motion, bringing her forehead crashing down on the deputy's nose. The deputy falls to the asphalt, stunned and bloodied. He looks up, blinking through the shock, only to see that Cheryl has retained control of his own sidearm, now leveling it squarely on him, centering the barrel on his forehead - all without the aid of eyesight to assist her aim. Struggling to breathe and maintain consciousness after the fierce blow, Cove weakly raises his hand and manages to mutter, "Cheryl... please...no."

Cheryl's grin spreads, revealing more crimson-stained teeth caging her severed tongue. She fixes her gaping, soulless eye sockets on the battered and bloodied deputy, gun trained on the broken man.

"DO-Om...Issss...HERE. YoUU...ArRrRe...DOoM." These are the last, clumsy words the matriarch of Springerville will speak with her severed tongue ...or rather, emit from within, before she turns the gun on herself and presses the muzzle to her temple. The spray of blood and gray matter splashes the black asphalt along with a clump of burgundy-dyed hair. The pistol drops from her grip, fingers adorned with shattered press-on nails releasing it, and Cheryl crumbles with a sickening thud onto the road. The timeline of this video feed cuts.

18

   Security Cameras, Lane 2: Wet Lab
   TOP-RIGHT QUADRANT OF THE SCREEN

The security camera pans the lanes of the wet lab, its motorized pan and tilt mount whirring quietly as the internal servos slowly and smoothly rotate the camera. The empty testing lanes appear clean and sterile at first. As the camera continues its lateral scan of the space, it slowly reveals new flecks of color. Splashes of dark red begin to brighten and grow into fresh and vibrant pools and shades of red. Then the color congeals into meaty, chunky pools of grisly texture.

Beneath the rows of sterile fluorescent lights suspended throughout the long room, the carcasses of a baboon and a convicted felon hang limp from their securing posts. The orange jumpsuit clings in tatters to the burnt and blistered corpse of the prisoner, while the fur of the baboon appears singed and smokes in patches that reveal blackened flesh. Trails of dark crimson lead from each corpse, and the faint trickle of their residual lifeblood can be heard as it flows down the small industrial drains set at the center of the room. A wet lab, indeed.

After a few moments, the camera centers, holds, and begins to pan back to the right. Screams echo in the distance, followed by sharp bursts of static and a thunderous crackling that causes the camera to flicker and the microphone to peak and cut out as it records the sound. Each time the noise emits, the lights in the wet lab dim. The chaos steadily increases in volume as the camera pans further to the right. One of the side entrance doors to the lab swings open violently. A group of scientists in lab coats charges into the room, screaming and shoving one another!

"Move! Go!!!" a female of the scientists in the rear of the pack screams in a shrill, terrified voice. Some of the labcoats stumble headfirst into the room, tripping others, while those with any athletic ability attempt to leap over their fallen colleagues, not stopping to assist them. It's pandemonium and every lab coat for themself. The leaders of the charge sprint ahead, making a beeline for the exit doors on the opposite end of the space. The hollering intensifies when their badges fail to change the electronic keypad from red to green, and they realize they have been trapped. The subtle buzzing crackle of electrostatic charging is followed by a snapping rip in the atmosphere as a tremendous release of energy shudders through the room: ZZZZZzzZzZzZzZZzzzzZZZ....CRACKLE-ZAP! A booming thunderclap follows, accompanied by screams and the flickering of overhead lights. Static interference appears on the security footage at the moment of electrical discharge, and the panic among the group of scientists increases.

"Fuck! He's coming! Who has a key!? Try yours! Who has the fucking override keys?! Hurry!" a pudgy male scientist screams.

The lab coats clamor at the door, pounding on it and attempting to kick it open. They must know that the place is engineered to adhere to top security clearance standards, making such efforts futile. However, this kind of irrational behavior is what panic induces - even in those with the highest IQs, such as these highly clinical and analytical employees of Dynamic Logistics, who now appear as terrified lambs to an impending slaughter.

"NO!!!" the female lab coat screams as the door across the room opens. She cowers and huddles behind her colleagues, shaking with fear as she clings to their backs, effectively using them as shields against the terror entering the room.

The terror: a middle-aged lab coat, youthful in appearance, Asian, male, stooped and slight in stature. He sort of resembles the Indiana Jones character, Short Round. By all standards of human physicality, he appears unassuming - stereotypically harmless, one might say. However, the man's lab coat and face are spattered with red. He wears a pair of welding goggles over his eyes, which are equally speckled with blood, but he appears calm and at ease while his colleagues scream and pound on the door across the wet lab in terror. He seems almost at peace. They are clearly not cowering because of his mere presence, per se, but rather because of what he has brought into the room with him.

Hanging at his side in one hand, he hefts the large, polished metallic device seen in previous footage - the lightning gun - which now shrouds his fist and forearm. The device emanates a bright, oscillating bluish light from a core within its midpoint. A pronged centrifuge spins slowly at the fore-end, near where his fist would be located within the enclosure. As the short scientist steps forward into the room, he pulls along a length of interlinked chain that rattles as he drags it. After pulling about six feet of chain, it is revealed to be connected to the collar of one of the test subject baboons.

One of the other female scientists shrieks loudly and collapses to her knees, pressing her back against the far wall near the locked exit doors as the pair steps forward. The baboon hoots in reply. Agitated and anxious, the primate cautiously moves alongside the short scientist, tugging lightly against the chain as it curiously peers around the room, focusing on the huddled scientists grouped together. The short scientist doesn't seem to pay it any heed. With each step closer, the cluster of lab coats cowering together huddles further into the corner of the wet lab, pleading and trying to use one another as cover.

"Oh God! Please, no. I - I have - children!" one of the men stammers.

"No, no, no, no..." another female scientist stammers.

The short, serene scientist towing his pet baboon stops next to the corpse of the convict in the tattered orange prison jumper and observes the slumped and shackled body tethered to the steel post. He slowly raises his hand holding the baboon's leash and removes his welding spectacles. As he does, blood trickles down his face from pools contained behind each heavily tinted eye cup. The once-white of his eyes are now saturated and dark with syrupy red blood. He slowly turns his grisly stare to the cowering mass of lab coats and begins to speak in a belching, bellowing volley of low, grumbling syllables.

"ShaAaaa-Me. ThISS BO-DdDddYYYYY...SUPERioR CoMPOsiTIOn." He leans down to examine the broken body of the convict, his face just inches from the twisted corpse. A silent moment passes, and then he turns to the scorched carcass of the baboon. After a few seconds of intense, almost robotic observation of the deceased primate husk, he rights himself and peers back at the gaggle of lab coats. "NExXxxXxXT Ti - MmmE" is the last thing he belches before dropping the chain to the ground and leveling the metallic hand apparatus downrange at his horrified coworkers. The glow from the device shrouding his arm intensifies, and a high-pitched whine can be heard on camera, increasing in volume.

"Fuck this!!!" one of the male lab techs yells before making a beeline downrange into the wet lab, trying to zigzag as he bolts across the room, his lab coat flapping behind him. The slight Asian scientist tracks him with his maroon eyes and drops the link of chain tethering him to the baboon. The scrambling scientists weaves his way through the wet lab and stumbles around the corpses, but his lack of athleticism and flat feet are no match for the primal speed and ferocity of the primate that Shorty has now unleashed from its chain. The flat-footed scientist makes it about ten feet before the baboon launches itself through the air, landing on his back with a sickening crunch, the mass of the beast pressing the air out of him in a strained and breathy wheeze. The screams of the huddled lab coats in the room's corner are almost loud enough to muffle the sound of ripping and tearing as the baboon effortlessly peels strips of flesh from the scientist's face with one hand while grasping and tearing his genitals clean off through the man's now-soiled khaki slacks.

Screams. Horror. Scrambling. The microphones distort from the volume of terror as the lens pans across the room. The remaining lab coats scatter and climb over one another like ants being evicted from their anthill after it has been doused with gasoline and set ablaze by a teenage pyro.

In this case, however, the fire is lightning. Spears of jagged blue, yellow, white, and sickening green lightning bolts crackle and flicker across the room. The blast of energy emanates from the directed energy weapon encasing Shorty's hand, the core glowing an intense bright white, the pronged gyroscopic end spinning in an accelerated blur, spitting waves of controlled lightning like threads of pure deadly energy from a supercharged loom.

The cowering female scientist using her colleagues as cover is among the first to ride the lightning. A large branch of blue light arcs and redirects, bouncing between the I-beams on the ceiling overhead before completing its circuit as a bolt skewers her head and reconnects through her torso. In a bright flash accompanied by a thunderous clap that shakes the room, her superheated insides paint the corner, thick black ash expelling in a cloud, and charred bits of her white lab coat flutter and fall to the ground in a burst of embers. All that remains of the young woman is a steaming pile of blackened entrails, tatters of pink flesh, and a melted plastic ID badge dangling from a lanyard.

All the while, Shorty's expression remains docile and pleasant as thunder continues to clap and the room shudders. In under thirty seconds, the remaining lab coats meet a swift and similar fate, leaving the wet lab glistening and filled with thickening grey smoke and ash.

22:03:55

Combined: Facility Security Cameras +
Laboratory Employee Body Cams: Multiple Source Angles, Condensed - 4K, 60fps

A series of kinetic and jumpy body cam videos play out. Security guards sprint down the facility hallways as klaxon alarms sound and security lights strobe, only to be assaulted and tackled viciously by rabid, blood-drenched lab coats who seem possessed and hellbent on tearing them to shreds. A gang of cybernetically altered baboons with VR visors and pulsing energy weapons clamped to their fists leap off the hallway walls, swing from light fixtures, and brutally dispatch the screaming scientists and janitorial staff members they encounter.

Another POV from a scientist in a robotics lab shows him scrambling for cover, crashing headfirst over a stainless steel equipment cart. A quadruped robotic dog clacks its metallic feet as it bounds forward and slides to a stop in front of the terrified man.

"Halt! Command halt! Code red, halt! HALT!!!" the lab coat shouts at the robot, but his voice has no effect as he backs into the room. The mechanical canine proceeds, undaunted by the commands, hunkering low as it articulates its pincer-shaped mechanical head and scans the scientist with a red laser light. The robot's movements create the illusion of sentience, embodying the traits of a true predator as it stalks forward. The gleaming pincer jaw opens and snaps shut with a metallic clang. The scientist flinches, backing up against a row of laboratory cabinets. As he trembles, the POV footage captures his shaking hands reaching for a stack of paper binders filled with documentation, which he tosses at the robot dog. The documentation scatters, and he lunges away from the mech, bounding between the sterile steel tables in an attempt to reach the other side of the room. The robot dog reacts instantaneously, its pincer head and servo-driven neck easily dodging the heavy binders while simultaneously priming its four piston-powered legs to propel itself atop a nearby cabinet, instantly regaining visual contact with the lab coat and pursuing him effortlessly. In a smooth action that takes under half a second to complete, a seamless compartment opens on the top of the robot's torso, and a foot-long barrel protrudes from the enclosure. A flash burst of automatic gunfire erupts from the mech's clandestine submachine gun. The lab coat's backside blossoms red, and he tumbles headfirst into a cart full of glass vials and equipment. Man's best friend: one. Humanity: zero. The timeline of this video feed cuts.

19

21:52:11
   4 Sources, Combined:
   AccuShot - Weapons Mounted HD Camera
   IRay MICRO 384 12 Micron 25mm Thermal Imager
   Canon R5 DSLR
   GoPro Hero 12 Black - Vehicle Mounted
   LOWER-LEFT QUADRANT OF THE SCREEN

The handheld camera focuses on the carcass of the downed feral hog as the trio of hunters approaches cautiously. The hog's dark bristles glisten in a pool of its own crimson blood.

"Holy shit, man, what was that?!" Steve exclaims as the echoes of thunder roll across the wide-open prairie.

"Heat lightning...maybe..." Mike mutters off camera.

"Did I get him?! Like, he's down, right?!" Connor, out of breath and excited from the thrill of his fresh kill, speaks with adrenaline still fresh in his trembling voice. Steve, holding the camera and documenting the hunt, lumbers forward to frame Connor in the shot.

"Easy, easy. Chamber a round, buddy. In case it's not out of the fight," Mike advises cautiously, taking the lead for the group with his rifle at the ready. Connor follows his instruction.

The camera zooms in on the carcass. The wind picks up, stirring wisps of dust and gently swaying the nearby brush. The thick bristles on the hog's bloodied backside move slightly in the breeze. The trio slows their approach as they draw closer to the massive feral hog.

"What do you think? Are we good?" Connor asks Mike.

Mike stands ready, raising his rifle and quickly aiming.

"Alright, Connor, put one right between its eyes now. Go ahead," Mike instructs calmly.

Connor raises his own rifle and aims down. The crack of his rifle discharging echoes as he fires another high-caliber round through the swine's skull. Mike turns back to the camera, relaxing with a grin. "With pigs, always remember to give them one for good measure. You can never be too safe with these thick-skulled bastards. Years back, we were on a hunt and dropped a four-hundred-pounder after plugging him with three rounds of 6.5 Creed before he stopped running. The swine still had enough fire in him to spring up on us and took a chunk out of my buddy TJ's calf. They really are tough - " Mike's hunting story is abruptly interrupted by a sickening popping and crunching sound behind him, like celery stalks snapping. He instinctively turns, rifle raised.

The camera focuses, capturing in the inky darkness the sight of bloody bristles moving, protruding bone glinting, chunks of meat falling, and drooping sharpened tusks. The pig is indeed moving, but not in any way natural to this earth or its creatures. Bluish sparks crackle along the hide of the fallen beast, making the thick hairs ripple. Its hindquarters spasm and contort, bones cracking as they splinter through the animal's thick skin, jutting out in sickening, jagged stabs.

IRay MICRO 384 12 Micron 25mm Thermal Imager

In the thermal imager, the outline of the hog is shrouded in cool colors. There is something flickering around the outline of the hog's form, however. Something warm based on the coloration of the thermal palette... The pig is ensconced in the flickering, transparent outline of a much larger quadruped of some sort. Hunched over and on all fours, you can distinctly make out the contours of four long legs, or appendages, and finger-like...claws. The screen quickly shows a side by side shot from the GoPro, which is mounted to Connor's backpack strap, and the thermal imager mounted on his rifle. The figure is not apparent on the GoPro...

"What...the hell..." Steve manages to choke out from behind the camera, steadying himself in front of the grotesque spectacle.

A bluish glow begins to emanate from the limp and shattered snout. The faint light intensifies, and a glimmer appears from behind its dead eyes, one of which dangles from the right socket of its broken skull.

Mike raises his rifle and fires three shots in rapid succession. Tufts of bristle and blood chunk off the animal, but it does nothing to stop its movement. More popping, crunching, and wrenching sounds erupt as the musculature beneath the pig's hide begins to swell, and it slowly starts to prop itself upright. The broken, bloodied beast turns its shattered snout and skull toward the men, gazing at them with the eerie pale blue light now pulsing from within its body.

"Run!!!" Mike yells at the top of his lungs to the others.

The monstrosity unleashes a deep bellow and lunges forward on its twisted haunches. The camera work becomes chaotic, bouncing wildly as Steve bolts from the scene. The trio of hunters can be heard yelling to one another, and then - BOOM! BOOM! The sound of a rifle firing off-camera is followed by the whoosh of rounds tearing through the air across the wide-open range.

The feed cuts to Mike's rifle scope camera. Dirt and dust erupt from the desert floor as rounds impact near the macabre swine charging toward him, its dislodged glowing blue eyeball bouncing wildly like an out-of-control wrecking ball. Mike fires one last shot just as the abomination leaps into the air, obscuring the frame in a blur. The scope camera then clatters to the desert floor. A moment later, Mike is seen scrambling on his hands and knees, only to be violently knocked aside as a blur of fur and tusks rams into his ribcage, pinning him to the ground. The gruesome, shattered snout of the beast rears up before bearing down on him as he struggles with his chest holster to regain control of his pistol. BOOM!

A single round from the .357 magnum revolver rips through the top of the hog's skull. In that instant, the bluish light from within the animal flickers and goes out. Blood from both the beast and Mike's fresh injuries saturates him as the animal slumps headfirst onto Mike's chest with a thud.

The scope camera footage cuts.

22:02:09

* * *

The GoPro mounted on the side-by-side crossbar films the interior of the off-road vehicle. Steve and Connor struggle to support Mike as they help him into the vehicle. Mike grunts in pain as he is loaded into the rear. Panicked, Connor and Steve toss their gear into the backseat. Steve jumps behind the wheel while Connor climbs into the back cabin to assist Mike.

"Med kit! Velcro'd to the back seat! Get the quick clot and those compression bandages on him now! Hang in there, buddy!" Steve exclaims as Connor searches through the first aid kit, using his headlamp for light.

Steve turns the ignition and fumbles with the GPS.

"Shit, shit. Fucking GPS isn't working. Which way - " he mutters, trembling as he pokes at the dashboard.

Mike leans forward, grunting in excruciating pain. He squeezes Steve's shoulder tightly, capturing his full attention. Pointing in a direction, he manages to say, "That way," before leaning back in his seat to catch his breath. Connor starts tending to his wounds.

"Right. Okay, buckle up and hold on, man. We're getting you out of here," Steve says, doing his best to maintain composure.

"What the fuck was that back there?" Connor exclaims, tearing open the plastic packaging of an Israeli quick-clotting bandage. He applies it with pressure to a bloodied wound on Mike's chest that is oozing blood.

Blue lightning erupts on the horizon behind them. Arcs of pale light dance across the desert floor in sporadic bursts, followed by what sounds like cannon fire. After the rumbling bass of thunder subsides, an eerie high-pitched sound pierces the air. It is unmistakable - the howling of wolves. A pack, not far away, is caught in a frenzy, fighting and yelping. Suddenly, the sounds of yelping and screeching emerge. Something is attacking the pack, and they are losing the battle quickly. Then...silence.

The men drive in silence, each straining to listen over the roar of the side-by-side engine for any danger lurking in the darkness. A volley of blue lightning illuminates the desert landscape behind them, followed by one last symphony of sound. Connor glances back at something on the horizon...or perhaps it's just the final flashes of rolling lightning playing tricks in the shadows across the rocky terrain.

The camera cuts.

Trail Camera: In complete darkness, the InfraRed view saturates the screen with a phosphorescent white light. The desert is still, save for a gentle breeze swaying the branch of a nearby creosote bush. Suddenly, a dark mass streaks past the camera at great speed, shaking the bush to which the camera is fixed. Moments later, another flash of fur and long, lunging limbs darts by, momentarily obscuring the wide-angle lens. Silence holds for ten seconds, then the low, plodding rumble of a herd moving in a pack grows louder. At least ten creatures bound through the frame, kicking up dust, followed closely by another twenty in tight formation, making it difficult to discern their exact number and identity. The infrared black-and-white view of the game camera offers little clarity in the moment. Amidst the mass of dark fur, blurred movements, and swirling dust, a few striking features stand out against the brighter parts of the image as they rush by. These white areas - claws, teeth, and bones - protrude from the thick gray and black fur coats, revealing the animals to be wolves.

As the main herd thins and disappears from view, one final wolf stops short, scanning the terrain before shifting its gaze robotically toward the trail camera. Although the camera is discreetly mounted and concealed within the bush, making it nearly invisible to the naked eye - especially at night - the wolf seems almost aware of its presence. In infrared mode, these cameras emit no visible light or sound, designed specifically to observe without startling or being detected by terrestrial creatures.

The lone wolf approaches the camera, releasing a low growl from deep within its throat. As it nears, its teeth are bared, and its eyes begin to emit an unnatural glow, unlike the typical infrared spectrum. Much like the feral hog, this wolf's eyes shine with an internal light. As it draws closer, its features come into sharper focus. The animal appears disheveled, with a stilted and rigid gait, reminiscent of one that has been struck by a vehicle. It seems broken yet retains a powerful and intimidating presence.

To emphasize its status as an apex predator, the wolf lunges at the trail camera, jaws open and snout snarled. In an instant, its teeth crush the plastic casing of the camera, and the feed cuts out.

Go Pro and AccuShot - Weapons Mounted HD Camera

Gunshots echo from Connor's rifle as the side-by-side swerves along a dusty desert trail, brake lights intermittently casting an eerie red glow through the swirling dust behind them. The footage is shaky and chaotic. The view steadies slightly as Connor aims at the cloud of dust trailing behind. "Go! Don't fucking stop!" he yells to Steve, .;in the driver's seat. Connor's rifle shifts nervously between two lunging shadows emerging from the dust - two wolves rapidly closing in. BOOM! He fires another round, but it has no effect on their pursuers. Grumbling from Mike can be heard in the edit as the GoPro angle reveals him slumped in the seat next to Connor, jostling with every turn, held in place only by his seatbelt. Beneath the safety harness, wads of soaked bandages struggle to stay in place. "Hold on, buddy! We're almost there!" Connor shouts to Mike. The menacing shadows grow larger with every leap behind the side-by-side, their long limbs casting even longer shadows. The flashes of light and shifting darkness distort these two unseen monsters, making their exact size, distance, and form hard to discern. Then, they begin to emerge from the choking dust. Enormous paws claw at the dry desert floor, ripping and tearing to gain ground on their prey. Through Connor's scope, we see them up close - eyes faintly glowing blue and snarled snouts oozing muddy, bloody mucus. BOOM! A tuft of fur and a chunk of flesh tear from one of the wolves, but it does nothing to slow its pursuit. "Hold on! Turning! Fuck! Oh fuck!" Steve shouts from the driver's seat.

In an instant, the cameras spin violently, their lenses shrouded in dust. After a cacophony of crashing and distorted sounds, they settle. The side-by-side has flipped, rendering the GoPro footage nearly useless. Connor's rifle scope cam lies nearby, buried in dirt. Only the audio remains to convey the chaos of the scene: gunfire, screaming, snarling, gnashing, and the sound of plodding and scraping. Then, the rifle scope cam is pulled from the dirt, shaking and moving again. BOOM! A flash of gunfire erupts, its bloom obscured in haze. Connor's wheezing can be heard as he runs. The scope cam steadies, and a hand reaches up to wipe the lens clean. The scene unfolds.

Fifty yards away, the side-by-side lies in a heap, overturned next to an embankment. It is ablaze, casting flickering orange light on a horrific sight. Steve is being devoured by one of the monstrous wolves in the middle of the trail, his entrails piled nearby while his limbs still writhe. He raises his arms in a final, desperate attempt at defense as the beast sinks its teeth into his sternum, tearing him apart without remorse. The other wolf perches atop the wrecked vehicle, its front haunches and long snout buried in the rear of the cab, viciously tearing at Mike's body. Connor steadies his aim, centering his shot on the torso of the beast. He fires. The wolf jolts and recoils, glancing back down the smoke-filled, dusty trail toward Connor before returning to its meal. Connor's scope cam slowly pulls back and begins to jostle as he makes a run for it.

20

   SPEC OPS Helmet Cams
   LOWER-RIGHT QUADRANT OF THE SCREEN

A soft chime pulses through the room.

The Arbiter's display flickers and then stabilizes. Multiple panes populate in sequence, each locking into place with seamless transitions. High-contrast interface elements flash as inbound data syncs to the feed. The Junior Arbiters have done their digging on the four soldiers providing security for General Dennings, with the advanced AI powering our search scrubbers serving as an effective tool despite how buried their backgrounds had been.

A notification pings at the top left of the screen:

SUPPORT PERSONNEL IDs: VERIFIED. CONFIRMATION PROCESSING...
   [Access Level: JUNIOR ARBITER | Field Intelligence Uplink]
   [Stream ID: ARES-ENC-77K | Dynamic Logistics Compound]
   IDENTITY MATCH: 4 SUBJECTS CONFIRMED
   1. SSG Marcus Wynn (Callsign: "Hawk")

Former Unit: 1st SFOD-D (Delta Force)

Role: Team Lead / Direct Action Commander

Confirmed operational deployments in Mogadishu, Idlib, and various unlisted operations throughout the Sahel and Caucasus. Recently transferred to CIA Task Force Phoenix under deep clearance. The last four years have focused on non-attributed black sector targeting. Field behavior: Mission-focused. Maintains composure under pressure. Exhibits innovative command improvisation with a perfect record in extractions. Contractor for Midnight Shadows Operations Group.

2. CPO Donovan Riggs (Callsign: "Bishop")

Former Unit: DEVGRU (SEAL Team 6)

Role: Second-in-Command / Technical Breach & Communications

Served as an embedded JTAC and rapid communications specialist during over 20 confirmed kinetic interdictions. Joined the covert assets division post-2021 with no-return clearance, believed to serve as an internal logic check for Wynn. Highly effective in close-quarters combat, demonstrating exceptional field awareness in low-visibility scenarios. Contractor for Midnight Shadows Operations Group

3. SFC Evan Cole (Callsign: "Sawyer")

Former Unit: 75th Ranger Regiment – Regimental Recon Company

Role: Overwatch / Long-Range Reconnaissance

Participated in advanced scout detachments and forward reconnaissance in Tier-1 theater environments. Recognized for his ability to execute silent perimeter collapses and fallback strategies during rapid retreats. Contractor for Midnight Shadows Operations Group

4. GySgt Raul Vega (Callsign: "Ox")

Former Unit: MARSOC – Marine Raider Battalion

Role: Heavy Weapons / Point Breach Assault

Assigned to high-lethality breach and suppression missions for CIA-related extraction. Specializes in structural denial, drone suppression, and shockwave tactics during first contact. Contractor for Midnight Shadows Operations Group

Sirens and alarms drone throughout the building at high volume, while strobing alarm lights spin and splash the corridor with yellow and red light. Screaming and gunfire echo down the hallways somewhere in the bowels of the building. The mercenaries move in perfect concert as they traverse the blood-stained hallways, with General Dennings protected at the center of their ranks. Dennings holds a pistol low and at the ready as the mercenaries level their rifles, scanning their respective sectors for threats. The expressions on the faces of these well-trained killers are what we call "locked in." This is what they have trained for and been bred for over multiple deployments and countless contract jobs across various theaters of war. This is their element.

"This way!" Hawk, the lead mercenary, gestures down a hall toward a series of double security doors. At the foot of the threshold, one of the installation's many scientific officers is slumped against the wall, his white lab coat soaked in blood, with a large swath of red smearing a trail from where his body was clearly dragged along the wall until it was dropped in a heap on the linoleum floor.

Hawk reaches down and strips the corpse's ID badge and security card from the lanyard, not skipping a beat as Donovan provides cover and scans the hall. General Dennings grimaces at the body on the ground, not so much in disgust but in disapproval and disappointment. The group moves again toward their objective. An explosion echoes from deeper within the mountain complex, halting the men as they take a moment to observe the corridors for movement and potential threats.

The helmet cam perspectives shift among all four soldiers, each covering a different angle at the four-way intersection where they stand. Hawk motions to Bishop, then quickly turns and swipes the key card in the doorway's magnetic security card reader. The red LED light turns green, and the *ka-chunk* sound of the magnetic locks disengaging echoes overhead. The door glides open, revealing a short corridor and the massive blast-proof doors leading to the helipad beyond. The team enters, and the security door closes behind them.

21:57:54
Helipad Security Cameras & Helmet Mounted Video

The soldiers and General Dennings jog to the helicopter at the center of the helipad. The sky is alight with rolling electrical storms, and dark clouds have rolled in on the horizon as far as the eye can see, surrounding the mountain.

The POV of Hawk as he approaches the aircraft bounces up and down until he reaches the sliding door of the helicopter and swings it open. The pilot, seated in the cockpit, turns to the soldier and seems agitated as he points to his headset to indicate he is attempting to communicate. The pilot flips a few switches off and then on within the console.

"I repeat, central command, we have lost all power. Critical systems are not responding. Comms are running on battery power only. Do you copy?"

General Dennings leans into the aircraft and addresses the pilot sternly. "Pilot. What's the situation?"

"Sir, we've lost all power. No joy getting any systems to respond or come back online. It's like they're completely fried."

"Aren't these birds hardened?! They can take a lightning strike and keep spinning…" Hawk barks as he and the rest of the security detail hold their rifles steady on the blast door. The pilot notices the demeanor of his counterparts for the first time and looks concerned.

"What the hell's going on, sir?" the pilot asks earnestly.

"Nothing good. The installation's compromised. We need to find an alternate point of egress," Dennings says commandingly.

22:01:07

The massive blast doors open yet again, and General Dennings, along with his security detail of mercenaries, enters the complex, now with the pilot in tow at the rear of their formation. Although the ceiling-mounted security alarm lights continue to strobe throughout the hallways, the sirens have now ceased their ringing in the cavernous labyrinth of corridors. Only a few steps into the complex, Hawk halts the team's movements by freezing in his tracks and holding up a fist.

"You hear that?" he asks the team.

"Quiet," Ox responds.

"Not a soul," Sawyer chimes in pensively from the rear of the pack.

"Shh!" Bishop hisses, silencing them all as they follow his gaze to the end of the hall.

The entire group listens silently. No gunfire. No screaming. No alarms. Only the faint sound of tapping. A rhythmic and staccato CLINK. CLINK. CLINK. CLINK. repeating over and over, slightly louder with each tap of what sounds like metal on concrete.

Hawk signals again, and the entire group moves forward toward a hallway intersection. The view from the head-mounted video camera captures his perspective as Hawk approaches the corners tactically, quickly leveraging his rifle around the corner to sight targets as needed. However, there are no standing targets down either hallway as viewed through the helmet-mounted cameras - only carnage.

Gore stains the hallways. Dripping meat leaks from the ceiling. Dead scientists lie piled atop one another, taken down while fleeing from something. Dead baboons with mechanized limbs, some severed from their bodies, are scattered about. Complex security guards are slumped in crimson-stained and torn uniforms. The walls are dotted and pockmarked with bullet holes and long scrapes in the concrete or exposed bedrock of the mountain.

Bishop scans the hallway for movement and approaches a pile of bodies. He halts short and waits for cover from Hawk before quickly kneeling before the corpses, examining them.

"Yo! We got a live one," Bishop exclaims, reaching down and moving one of the bloodied bodies aside.

From Bishop's POV camera we see the body of Anika Das, from the neural interface division, huddled beneath the pile. Bishop grabs her shoulder and shakes it. The young woman, spattered in the blood of her fallen colleagues, trembles. She clutches fiercely to a locket hanging from her neck that is entangled with her ID badge.

Bishop moves the corpses off of her.

"Dr. Das, are you injured?" Bishop says, studying her name badge. The young scientist looks up, terror in her eyes.

"N-no," she manages. Bishop quickly pulls her from the pile of bodies and examines her. No wounds, no leaks.

"We gotta move. Can you walk?" he asks. She nods and he helps her to her feet.

"We don't have time for this shit. We gotta roll." Sawyer says off camera. Marcus monitors the hall, rifle steadied. He quickly gestures for the team to hold position, hearing something in the distance.

Aside from the faint crackling of fires burning, the only sound captured on the cameras is the steady mechanical metallic metronome growing louder from somewhere difficult to pinpoint within the complex. CLINK. CLINK. CLINK. CLINK.

"What the hell, man..." the pilot exclaims.

Das' eyes widen in horror.

"No...no..no," she begins to say before Bishop silences her with his gloved hand.

CLINK. CLINK. CLINK. CLINK. The sound intensifies. The soldiers scan the halls with their rifles. CLINK. CLINK. CLINK. CLINK. The sound grows louder, and then the source reveals itself far off at the end of the long, tunnel-like hallway.

The soldiers turn, weapons dipping slightly as they lock on to the glistening metal apparatus, its surface streaked with slick red residue. Low to the ground, with four metallic, piston-driven claws, it resembles a variation of the robotic attack dog that has turned on humans before - only this one is different. A significant modification distinguishes it from its predecessor. Mounted on its back is a rotary cannon, a miniaturized version of the minigun, more accurately referred to by its original designation: the Gatling gun.

"Move!" Marcus bellows as he turns, and the minigun spins, immediately erupting, ripping a line of destruction down the hall as it strafes while locking on to its ultimate target. The walls of the hallway explode, the immense rate of fire impacting and sending shards of granite and concrete flying like shrapnel as the rounds hone in on their target.

Bishop yanks Dr. Das to her feet and begins to push her away from the chaos. A mere second later, General Dennings' body goes sailing as his chest erupts in a geyser of blood from a volley of bullets. The deafening roar of gunfire subsides for a mere second as the cannon on the back of the dog pivots a few inches, refocusing its aim, and then it erupts once more. The pilot, Ox, and Sawyer are systematically cut in half in a cacophony of whirring gunfire, narrowly missing Hawk, Bishop and Das.

They scramble around the corner of the hallway and take cover, looking at each other in a daze. The gunfire ceases, and spent shell casings tinkle off the concrete floor. Then, a brief moment of complete silence before... CLINK. CLINK. CLINK. CLINK.

Bishop steels his resolve and strips a grenade from his battle belt. Hawk nods to him, and he pulls the pin, letting it fly around the corner blindly.

BOOM! The blast sends debris and roof tiles flying back down the hall near their position. Silence for a moment... then... CLINK... CLINK... CLINK... CLINK...

The three survivors run for it as their body camera feeds bounce with each step.

The feed cuts.

WORLDS COLLIDE

PART SEVEN

21

SPEC OPS Helmet Cams

The feed begins playing helmet cam footage taken from within an armored troop transport. The dark red interior light, designed to mitigate visibility from afar at night, casts an eerie hue over the scene. The helmet cam quickly spins and settles on the dash of the vehicle as Hawk removes it and settles back into his seat.

He is sweating profusely, and the new angle provides a wide view of the transport's interior and its three occupants. In the driver's seat is Bishop, and in the back seat, cradling her arms, is Dr. Das. Disheveled, with her head now wrapped in a blood-soaked bandage, she rocks slightly in her chair clutching her locket.

"Hey. You okay back there? What's your name?" Hawk snaps his fingers to get her attention and shake her from her trance. She looks at him vacantly.

"Anika." is all she can muster.

"I'm Hawk. This is Bishop," he says, nodding to the driver. "We're gonna get you out of here, you're gonna be okay. Are you injured? What can you tell us about what happened back there?" he asks.

"I need to get home. My kids." Das says, slowly opening the locket strung over her stained lab coat. Inside the locket, she reveals a photo of her and two young children. She transfixes on the image of her kids.

Bishop looks at Hawk skeptically. "How did we become a civilian rescue?"

Hawk shakes his head and hands back a bottle of water. Das' auburn hair is matted with blood and she's clearly in shock. Hawk resigns himself to gently setting the water on the seat beside her.

"Water, on the seat if you want it," he says, holding up his hands as he turns back to Bishop. "How far out?" he asks.

Bishop flips down a small cellphone navigation screen mounted to the front of his body armor, revealing a GPS map.

"Ten mikes," he says, inferring they are "ten miles" to their destination in military parlance.

"What the hell, man... What was that back there?" Hawk sighs, pressing his matted hair back and running his fingers through it.

"Tech gone haywire. I told my guys back in the day when the defense contractors were fuckin' around with all that autonomous bullshit, it was going to be the end of us - one way or the other. Welp, point in fucking case, brother. Fuck these egghead dipshits... Smoked fuckin Cole and Vega, man! Not to mention fuckin' Dennings. Oh Jesus... We're never going to hear the end of this, man. Mission's fubar. The General was about as high profile as they come. We ain't never being invited back to the party after this shit," Bishop laments as he wrings the steering wheel.

"Yeah, well, I have some shit to say to the brass back at HQ myself. This threat assessment had us prepped for any outward-facing assaults and attempts to intercept. Didn't expect to be ambushed by our own tech in a class-three facility, especially from inside the goddamned castle. And that's another thing, brother. The tech I get. Shit goes haywire, sure, maybe. Hacked? Who the fuck knows? But what in the holy hell was that shit in the testing lab? Asian broad, she went full demonic schizo during their little light show. I've seen some gacked-out Afghanis do some wild shit on brown brown, and I've seen some dudes from the hood take a bunch of hollow points from the cops and keep running, high on PCP and shit...but the way she lifted that dude's ass up in the air?! She weighed what, a buck, buck twenty? And then... did what she did to him. What the fuck, man..."

"Don't ask, don't tell... and you can bet whatever the fuck that was, they ain't gonna tell us a damn thing in the after-action report. It wasn't right, though...Cole and Vega man, that ain't no way to go out." Bishop says, staring down the road ahead, his eyes cold, flitting occasionally to the rearview mirrors, scanning the dark roadway as he drives.

Hawk sits up and leans forward in his seat, something catching his eye through the windshield far ahead.

The two commandos sit silently, contemplating their surroundings. From the perspective of Bishop's helmet-mounted camera, we see through the windshield of the troop transport vehicle. The intermittent white divider lines stitch the dark roadway in a steady rhythm as they speed into the seemingly endless black abyss of night. Desert scrub brush lines the edge of the black asphalt two-lane highway, and occasionally, a tumbleweed blows across the vehicle's path, indicating that the wind outside is still gusting in anticipation of the storm front. Beyond that, not much of the desert landscape can be discerned. However, many miles away, a faint orange glow is visible on the horizon. Following the road as a line of sight, the flicker of unmistakable firelight pulses gently in the distance.

"Yo, check it. Is that..." Hawk begins.

"Our destination. Springerville. Yeah."

"Fuck," Hawk says blandly.

"Fuck indeed," Bishop responds in kind.

Hawk picks up his helmet and places it back on his head, readying himself for whatever lies ahead.

23:40:27
SPEC OPS Helmet Cams

Flame engulfs the pharmacy and most buildings flanking Main Street, casting wild, flickering light across the chaos. Hawk turns, peering through the thick polycarbonate of his bulletproof passenger window. Twenty feet ahead, along the sidewalk, two disheveled women claw and climb over a sedan that has crumpled its front end against a telephone pole. Inside, a man struggles, his dog barking frantically - trapped in the vehicle. The women stop for a brief moment, turning to glance at the transport vehicle as it rolls by, their eyes dimly glowing blue.

"Weapons check," Bishop says methodically.

Hawk manipulates his rifle and checks the chamber, swapping out the current magazine for a fresh one. "Check," he responds.

From the backseat, Das whimpers. Hawk turns and addresses her calmly yet commandingly.

"Ma'am, you're going to be alright. This vehicle is like a bank vault on wheels; no one's getting in, and we're going to get out of here, okay? Just hang in there."

Das curls up, lifting her feet from the floor of the vehicle and cradling herself in a near-fetal position within the seat.

"Keep going. Let's head toward the center; there's got to be a PD or civic center there," Hawk says. Bishop follows instructions and turns the next corner, encountering more destruction along the way.

As soon as he rounds the corner, he slams on the brakes. An overturned school bus, the interior engulfed in flames, blocks nearly the entire street ahead. The road is littered with bodies - small, lifeless forms mixed with others writhing in agony, their bodies smoldering on the asphalt.

"Jesus Christ... those are kids," Bishop whispers.

"Can we go around?" Hawk asks, his voice hollow.

"We have to help them. We need to - " Bishop stammers, losing his composure until Hawk grips his arm, refocusing him.

"We aren't even here, brother. Like you said. You know the deal. Focus on the mission." The sternness in Hawk's eyes is unmistakable. Bishop nods slowly.

Amid the wailing and crackling sounds outside, the piercing screech of rubber on pavement suddenly fills the air behind them. A moment later, a gasoline tanker truck careens over an embankment, shuddering as it rumbles across the road, and slams into a nearby red brick building. The explosion sends a massive fireball into the sky and scatters bricks and debris throughout the area. The armored vehicle shakes with the low rumble of the explosion as blazing fragments rain down around them, peppering the hood of the transport.

"No egress. We can't push through. We're pinned down here," Bishop says, putting the vehicle in park and exchanging a knowing look with Hawk. Hawk turns to Das, sitting in the rear and shakes her knee.

"Hey! I know you're scared, but we need to get out of here now. We'll keep you safe, but I'm not carrying you, got it? It's time to move."

She reluctantly nods, clutching her necklace.

22

Connor's face fills the frame in the iPhone video, vacant stare scanning the horizon before him. Smudges of dirt streak his brow, sweat drips down his face, and his forearms are scraped and bruised. He runs his hands back through his disheveled hair, clearly worse for wear and out of breath. After taking a deep breath, he chokes up momentarily but quickly composes himself and begins to speak to the camera.

"Jamie, I'm a mile outside of Springerville, baby. I tried calling you. God, I've tried calling. There's no damn signal out here. Listen, if anything happens - if anything happens to me, sweetheart, I want you to know that I tried to reach you and get home to you and the kids. I love you all so much. Mike and Steve... they uhh,...they...fuck..." He chokes up and then composes himself. "They didn't make it, baby. Something horrible is out here in the desert. The wolves, they're rabid and something's got into 'em...and the feral pigs, Jesus, they aren't right. I don't know what it is. They attacked us and the side-by-side flipped and - I tried to get them out, baby. Right now, I just need you to know I love you and I am coming home to you. I promise I am going to try to- " Connor's words are cut off by the high-pitched howling in the not-so-far-off distance.

His face goes pale. He looks at the camera and remains still as the howling fades away.

"I'm coming home."

The iPhone video feed cuts.

00:36:21 - 09/23/22
AccuShot - Weapons Mounted HD Camera

The view through the AccuShot scope flickers, initially blooming with the firelight dotting the nearby ridge. Connor's voice is picked up by the camera's small onboard microphone.

"My god..." he whispers as he scans the horizon with his rifle, using the optic's variable power zoom to get a closer view of the chaos unfolding in the town below. The reticle hovers over buildings engulfed in fire. He pans across the town, surveying the roads littered with wreckage. Bodies lie limp in pools of dark liquid on the nearby sidewalks, while others are strewn about in the streets, limbs in unnatural and contorted positions. An LED range-finding metric appears in the corner of the screen, indicating that the building on the edge of town is 0.5 km away.

He pans the scope along the chaotic streets a bit further before coming to a stop, steadying the reticle. Movement catches his eye - a silhouette of a man shrouded in the smoke billowing from a nearby car fire. The distorted shadow lengthens and shifts as it moves through the haze, dragging one leg behind it. Injured, perhaps. As the figure advances and the smoke begins to clear, the shadow shortens and it comes into focus: a chacma baboon. With one augmented cybernetic leg and an armored, weaponized forearm cannon, the baboon meanders into the street, slowly turning its head from right to left, scanning its surroundings through the lenses of a VR visor bolted to its skull.

IRay MICRO 384 12 Micron 25mm Thermal Imager

The baboon's heat signature is almost white hot in the center. This beast has been burning some calories and is painting a hot signature against the cool desert night air. But it's the looming flicker of another form around the primate, a warm glowing silhouette that's most interesting. Standing on two appendages is a much taller form... flickering in and out on screen. As if the heat signature of whatever is behind it...or a part of it...is phasing in and out of existence on the thermal camera, somehow between planes of detectable existence.

A dog barks nearby. Suddenly, the animal turns and bolts across the street, leaping over a parked jeep and into a nearby alleyway. The sound of clattering is followed by primal howling and barking, paired with distant screams. Intense flashes of electric blue light emanate from the corridor. The dog yelps and the screams abruptly cease, and the echo of their last cries reverberates across the desert.

The feed cuts.

00:52:51 - 09/23/22

The scope camera scans Main Street from ground level. Connor has taken up a position on a sidewalk near the main intersection behind a raised cinder block flower bed. No movement is visible in the streets, but the flickering firelight casts shadows that create a fluid scene. It's difficult to determine whether the shadows are shifting or if something sinister lurks in the darkness. The image bounces as he runs and takes new cover behind an old beat up Chevy truck. The angle stabilizes as he braces his rifle along the top of the vehicle's hood, holding steady as he sights down the long stretch of road leading into the town center, where carnage sprawls in every direction. The only sounds are the crackling of fire consuming structures and distant alarms wailing somewhere in the haze. The rifle scope jiggles slightly as he manipulates the bolt and checks the chamber. Connor dashes forward, moving quickly, his labored breathing echoing with each step as he bolts down the road. Firelight dances on shattered storefront windows. He ducks into a doorway and scans the interior of a completely ravaged bar. Stools and shards of glass bottles litter the floor, but no bodies or patrons occupy the interior. He steadies the rifle again, panning down the rubble-strewn Main Street as he catches his breath and zooms the optic as far as it will go. Through the thick, curling black smoke, he spots a building at the end of the road. The lettering "SPRINGERVILLE POLICE DEPARTMENT" becomes visible. The structure appears intact, and the range finder displays "0.25k."

"Okay...let's go. You got this," Connor reassures himself.

The image jostles and bounces as he resumes his trek along the buildings, navigating around an abandoned sedan.

He hurries down the road, slowing as he approaches a burned-out minivan. A small girl, maybe eight or nine years old, is huddled near a body lying on the ground. Muffled cries escape her lips as Connor cautiously approaches her; her nightgown is soiled and tattered, singed from the fire.

"Hey... hey, you okay?" he whispers gently as he approaches her, trying to keep his voice low. As he approaches the young girl, she appears to be poking at the body, trying in vain to wake what must be her mother. From the sight of the crumpled figure, it's clear that the mother has succumbed to her injuries. Connor steps closer and leans down. The young girl turns her head, and he stops dead in his tracks. Her eyes glow with the familiar blue hue he has seen before. Her lips are twisted into an unnatural, devilish grin, half of her face mottled and blistered from burns.

"WE WiLL KiLL YoU ALLLL. YOU KnOW tHiSssss???" the child hisses up at him.

In her hands, she clutches a dagger of twisted, rusted metal. Blood drips down her arm, with bone and sinew exposed beneath her tattered flesh. Connor recoils in horror, stepping back as she contentedly resumes poking and plunging the shard into the corpse at her feet.

Connor runs, breath ragged and trembling, dodging debris as he bolts full tilt down the hellscape of Main Street.

Then - he stops short, skidding and tripping over his own feet as a flurry of matted fur and gleaming metal slams to the ground twenty feet in front of him.

The cyborg primate slides onto the roadway, kicking up dust upon impact and planting its thick knuckles firmly into the pavement. Grinding its teeth, it unleashes a guttural roar as it comes to a stop. Connor gasps loudly, and the reticle of his rifle attempts to stabilize on the macabre form. He fires a shot - BOOM! The round glances off the baboon's metallic shoulder plate, sparking and violently knocking its torso back. The glowing digital visor bolted to its thick skull briefly glimpses to its side to assesses the impact site before gnashing its teeth and glaring directly back down the road at Connor.

"Shit," Connor utters as the image shakes, and the sound of the bolt in his rifle actuating is heard on camera, brass tinkling from the spent shell hitting the pavement at his feet. The animal leaps forward, closing the distance and bellowing a howl that pierces the air. Connor stumbles back, the frame bouncing as he tries to regain his composure and aim once more, the baboon closing in at an incredible rate every time the scope cam catches a glimpse. The beast's thick hair obscures its form, but the musculature beneath its hide ripples as it bounds forth angrily. Connor falls back, his feet visible in the frame as he fires another round. BOOM! The high-powered shot misses completely as the creature hurls itself, unharmed, through the air.

"NOOO!" Connor screams, his voice echoing what would be his final word as the animal descends, mere feet away from delivering a hammer-fisted death blow with its glowing metallic arm cannon.

CRACK! The baboon's chest blossoms in a geyser of blood and fur, its torso thrusting backward from the impact. The cyborg primate lands with a thud on the pavement, its outstretched grasp going limp, hairy knuckles dragging on the road, outstretched fingers curling just inches from Connor's boots. Gravely injured, the creature's head adorned with the glowing visor lifts slowly, canine teeth glistening red, as it raises the humming cannon, preparing to take a shot at the now hyperventilating Connor. The scope cam trembles on the animal.

CRACK! Another round, fired from the unseen source, splits the visor dead center, shattering the glass enclosure and ripping the baboon's skull apart. Fur, metal, and brain matter separate and spray the street in glistening streaks as the beast goes limp. Connor's heaving breath is soon overtaken by the soft plodding of combat boots approaching from behind him.

"Target down. Hold perimeter," Hawk says, his boot steps echoing down the deserted street. "You good?" he asks as he enters the frame with Das in tow behind him.

"Yeah… yeah, I think so," Connor responds, still dazed.

"Good. On your feet. We're exposed out here." Hawk extends a gloved hand to help Connor up.

"Close one," Bishop says nearby, entering the frame with Das cowering behind him, one hand resting on his shoulder.

"This way." Hawk gestures toward the entrance of a nearby mechanic's garage. He shatters the window on the door, unlocks it, and rips it open, allowing the four survivors to take shelter inside.

"What the fuck is going on?!" Connor sputters as they close the door behind them, while Bishop scans the street through a window with his assault rifle.

"Nothing good. Whole town's fucked. We gotta find better cover," Hawk says commandingly.

"The PD. Edge of town. It looks like it's still okay," Connor says meekly.

"Where?" Hawk asks, his tone serious.

"About half a mile that way." Connor points toward the direction of the police station.

"Okay, that's our target. They should have emergency backup power and communications, if we're lucky. Our shit's all blacked out. You good to move?" Hawk asks, rummaging through a nearby mini fridge to retrieve bottles of water from behind the receptionist desk, handing them out to each person. Connor nods, eyeing the window wearily.

"Drink up. We leave in two minutes if the road is clear."

23

01:02:37 9/23/22
Police Cruiser Samsara MVARS Dash Cam
AXON Body Camera: POV Deputy Cove - 4K, 60FPS

The view from Deputy Cove's cruiser dash cam is a rollercoaster ride through Dante's Inferno.

Red and blue strobe lights pulse frantically, their chaotic flashes illuminating the fire-scorched town streets and buildings flanking them, creating a hellish landscape of light and shadow. The siren wails at full blast, drowned out by the relentless roar of the inferno consuming the town.

Cove's strained voice crackles through the CB radio.

"Anyone, this is Deputy Cove! Goddamnit! Springerville PD! We have a full-scale mass casualty event here! Need assistance! EMS and fire evacuation required, pronto! I repeat, Springerville PD - the town is under some sort of attack! Phone lines are down! Is anyone out there?!"

Silence and static.

The transmitter slams against the dashboard.

The cruiser banks hard, swerving to avoid the burned-out husk of a

169

school bus. The tires bounce violently over the curb as it careens around wreckage - multiple bodies lay strewn across the pavement, mangled and motionless.

Then - a wall of smoke ahead.

Cove plows forward, barely able to see through the thick, choking haze.

Screech!

The cruiser lurches to a stop.

Something large is blocking the road ahead.

Through the smoke, a massive tractor looms, its rusted bucket raised high, a blinding spotlight mounted on the cab slicing a beam of blinding light through the haze. The beam refracts in the swirling smoke, casting long, shifting shadows across the street and illuminating the wreckage in unnatural contrast.

As the smoke clears, twisted features become more distinct. Wedged between the jagged metal teeth and heaped within its scoop lies a writhing, twisted mass of bodies. Their vacant, glassy eyes pulse dimly with a sickly blue hue, reflecting eerily in the artificial glow.

At the wheel sits a scrawny, sinewy old farmer, his coveralls caked in mud and blood. His face is slack and lifeless, his eyes also alight with the sickening soft blue glow - pale and vacant.

Cove stares, frozen, his breath catching in his throat.

The farmer turns his head, shifts the tractor into gear, and slowly drives on. The tractor lumbers forward, hoisting its grotesque cargo toward a burning structure. Cove sits in shocked silence, breathing heavily.

The tractors treads rumble forth up and over the sidewalk and then - impact.

The tractor crashes into the inferno, plowing forth into the building as if it were made of wet cardboard, its rusted frame almost instantly swallowed by the escaping fire. The building groans and then collapses around it, sending a tidal wave of ash, cinders, and dust billowing up into then lights sky and littering the street with embers.

Cove exhales.

"Jesus Christ."

Then - gunfire.

POP-POP-POP!

Sparks spray across the hood.

"Shit!" Cove shouts as his rear driver's-side window explodes inward.

Muzzle flashes continue to light up from a nearby rooftop.

The bursts of gunfire reveal the shooters - men and women with eyes emanating the same sickly, unnatural blue. Their movements are eerily calm and methodical - no fear, no hesitation, no rush. Just cold, steady, relentless intent.

The body cam feed jerks violently as Cove ducks, shielding himself in the driver's seat. Glass rains down around him. He grips his sidearm, pops up to aim, and he returns fire.

Pop! Pop! Pop! His rounds ricochet and pepper the roofline. The assailants do not duck for cover however. They stare down, almost as if they were curious about their prey below. Cove ducks for cover as they aim on him once more.

BOOM!

A thunderous shot cracks through the still night air - not from the rooftop though.

Dead ahead.

A new threat.

A spout of steam erupts from the engine compartment as the round slams into the cruiser's hood.

Then - CLANK. CLANK. CLANK. CLANK. In front of the cruiser in a pool of light from a nearby streetlamp, the long gleaming stainless steel 30mm rifle barrel comes into focus first. Then, out of the shadows, the steel chassis of the enemy.

One of the robotic dogs.

BOOM!

Its mounted cannon smokes, and the mechanical frame shudders slightly from the recoil. Cove's headrest explodes in a puff of upholstery. The mech's twin optic sensors mounted to its head scan for the next target, rotating with eerie, mechanical precision.

BOOM!

Then - a sharp hiss.

The cruiser sinks slightly.

Blown tire.

POP! POP! POP!

Rounds riddle the cruiser, hammering the frame from above. The rooftop shooters have resumed firing on Cove. The activity appears to draw the attention of the robot dog, its head snapping upright and locking onto their rooftop position almost instantly.

The machines torso pivots followed by its legs.

Its targeting system locks on to the rooftop crowd.

BOOM! BOOM! BOOM! BOOM!

The 30mm cannon belches hellfire, ripping apart the red brick façade and punching clear through. The bodies of the townspeople disintegrate, tissue and bone tearing from them as if they were paper dolls.

One of the women aiming down at Cove's cruiser takes a round beneath her neck.

Her head separates instantly.

Red mist plumes into the air as her hair whips wildly, the severed skull flipping end over end. Glowing blue eyes spin through the darkness before toppling onto the pavement with a wet, sickening thud.

Cove sits upright, hands gripping the wheel.

No time.

He slams on the gas.

The cruiser lurches forward, tires screeching as he tears down the road.

The mechanized death dog jerks its pincer head toward him, tracking his movement.

The 30mm cannon begins to rotate - half a second too late.

Cove doesn't slow down.

BAM!

Impact.

Screeching metal, a violent explosion of parts.

Robot roadkill.

Seconds later, the police station comes into view.

The smoking, bullet-riddled cruiser skids into the lot.

Cove lunges for the shotgun, yanking it from its dash mount. His other hand grabs a loaded duffel marked with an emergency cross.

He bolts out.

The body cam footage bounces violently with each pounding step.

Then - movement - silhouetted figures appear at the edge of the frame.

Cove pivots, shotgun raised.

Four figures are closing in.

"BLUE! BLUE!" Hawk yells - a universally understood law enforcement and military callout, signaling "friendly" to avoid being shot in the chaos.

Cove keeps his aim steady, panting.

Hawk, Connor, Bishop, and the Das sprint forward.

"We ain't one of those things, man - we're good. Stand down!" Hawk shouts, raising one hand. Bishop covers their group, aiming his rifle at Cove, prepared to defend. Connor scans the streets, rifle drawn.

A tense standoff ensues.

"We need cover, boss!" Bishop warns, continuing to survey the street.

Deputy Cove eyes Das and Connor and lets his guard down a bit.

"You - the gas station earlier?" Cove asks Connor.

It takes Connor a second to process but he remembers his encounter earlier at the onset of the hunting trip.

"Yeah, yeah me and my…" Connor looks defeated remembering his friends.

At the edge of Main Street, shadowy figures begin to emerge from the smoke, their outlines flickering in the distance and growing clearer in Cove's peripheral vision.

More of them.

Glowing blue eyes pierce through the darkness.

No time to waste.

Cove lowers his shotgun, shaking off the adrenaline.

"Okay, inside. Move!"

The team converges and pushes into the station.

The deadbolt locks behind them.

EVACUATION ORDER

PART EIGHT

24

   Springerville Police Station Security Cameras - 4K, 60FPS
   SPEC OPS Helmet Cams
   AXON Body Camera: POV Deputy Cove - 4K, 60FPS
   AccuShot - Weapons Mounted HD Camera

*The footage from multiple camera angles is intercut seamlessly between subjects beyond this point.

   Cove closes and locks the cell door where the old drunkard had been detained. The cinder-block wall beyond the iron bars is caved in by the pickup truck, creating a fractured hole that frames the flickering chaos outside. Bishop takes position, rifle ready, keeping watch for movement through the opening, steel bars providing a barrier.

   "I almost shot you out there. Where the hell did you come from - the mountain? Are you military?" Cove asks Hawk, his speech fast and shaky as he sizes him up.

   "Something like that," Hawk replies steadily, glancing at Das. "We're trying to get out, and we could really use your help."

   "Well, that's just great. The whole town's on fucking fire! People I've known my entire life are shooting at each other - and me! Not to mention whatever the hell that thing was in the street. So, if you don't mind telling me exactly what's going on, that would be great!" Cove's voice cracks, the stress and adrenaline of the last ten minutes finally catching up with him.

Bishop turns to Cove, holding his rifle low but at the ready, still guarding the street opening. He exchanges a look with Hawk, who motions for him to stand down. Cove wrings his hands in frustration, then moves to a nearby desk and collapses into an office chair, quickly opening and closing the drawers in search of something.

Das retreats to the corner of the room, exhausted, cradling her head in her hands and clutching her locket. Hawk scans the room, spots the CB radio in the corner, and approaches Deputy Cove.

"Look, you know as much as we do. If we can get communications out, we can call for a rescue. I'll level with you, Officer - " he glances at Deputy Cove's badge. " - Cove. It seems like something far beyond our pay grades has gone wrong out here, and all we know is we need to exfil this area. We need to get a signal out, and fast." Hawk speaks coolly, calmly, and commandingly to Cove. "Are you tracking?"

Cove takes a deep breath and nods. Hawk gestures toward the nearby CB radio. "Does that thing work? My guy here can try to get a line out to a nearby unit and - " he begins, but Cove interrupts.

"It's dead. Just like the one in the cruiser. It started malfunctioning maybe an hour before all this chaos began. I thought the antenna on the roof might be damaged again, but I'm not sure..." Cove replies, slamming a desk drawer shut before opening another, rifling through papers and supplies in a frantic search for something.

"Yeah, same here. The phone's useless. Ever since the lightning strike, I haven't been able to get a signal," Connor adds from across the room.

"What's your story?" Hawk asks Connor.

"Me? Uhh...me and my buddies were hunting a few miles outside of town. We met the deputy before we left town. Then out there in the desert, this electrical storm hit, never seen anything like it. Right after, we were attacked. My friends..." Connor says.

"Attacked?" Hawk prompts.

"Yeah... first pigs, then... wolves. But they weren't right. Their bones, the way they moved... and their eyes... they were - " Connor trails off as Cove finishes his sentence.

"Blue. Glowing blue," Cove says, looking up from the desk drawer holding a key ring.

"What's with her?" Cove asks, nodding to Das, who is still huddled in a ball by the back wall, rocking herself.

"Scientist from that lab I think. She's cooked, man. We rescued her on our way out from that fucking lab. She was the only one - only one that wasn't DOA, completely fucked up… or taken over by this shit," Bishop says coldly keeping his eyes intently trained on the holding cell.

Cove raises an eyebrow. "So, you *were* at the lab, and you don't know what the hell this is?" he demands of Das. She remains silent, only tightening her grip on her legs and continuing to rock back and forth.

"Told you, man. Cooked," Bishop says dryly.

"Alright, everyone, let's fucking focus here. You said you have an antenna on the roof?" Hawk asks Cove.

"Yeah, but I'll be damned if I'm going up there. Already been shot at by half the town while climbing around on Main Street roofs tonight. I want to make sure I can shoot back," Cove says, holding up the keys. "Look…it appears you fellas can handle your own - even if I suspect you know more than you're letting on - and I don't know if I can make it back down Main Street alone. Our armory has ammo and supplies. If we stick together, maybe we have a better chance of getting the hell out of here. The nearest town is fifty-five miles away, and I don't want any of that trouble following us."

"Okay. Five meter target everybody. We need to check comms and get out of here. The antenna's elevation might be enough to break through and monitor chatter. Bishop, let's use our gear to try to boost the signal and send out an SOS. Let's see if we can get anything at all," Hawk suggests. Bishop nods in agreement.

"Cove…do your thing and get what you can from the armory and pack it up. Keep an eye on that hole. We're sitting ducks in here, so let's regroup in ten minutes. Everyone copy?" Hawk instructs.

"Copy," Cove replies.

01:47:17 09/23/22
SPEC OPS Helmet Cams

From the roof of the police department, the entire horizon glows orange with firelight from the surrounding structures. Hawk and Bishop approach a large metal antenna and junction box. Hawk quickly pries open the access cover, sets down his backpack, and removes a small communications controller, unspooling a short series of cables. He flips on his red headlamp helmet attachment and begins working, while Hawk scans the surrounding rooftops with his rifle.

Down below, a few townspeople shuffle aimlessly in the street, their eyes glowing. Hawk aims his rifle at them but refrains from firing. "Status?" he asks quietly.

"We've got power. Stand by for comms check," Bishop replies as he puts on a pair of small headphones and starts connecting the wires.

"This is Bravo-Charlie-Nine out of Springerville. Come in, Delta Three Overwatch, do you copy? We need rapid extraction. I repeat, this is Bravo-Charlie-Nine. Do you copy, Delta Three Overwatch?" Bishop speaks into the throat mic, the faint crackle of static breaking the silence. He inputs information into the handset controller and repeats his call.

"This is Bravo-Charlie-Nine out of Springerville. Come in, Delta Three Overwatch, do you copy?"

Static crackles again, followed by a series of audible digital clicks. CLICK. CLICK. CLICK.

"We need rapid extraction. I repeat, this is Bravo-Charlie-Nine. Do you copy, Delta Three Overwatch?"

CLICK. CLICK. CLICK.

Then, through the static, a faint voice responds, "This is Delta Three Overwatch. Operator, verify comms code."

"Zero-two-zero-nine-zero-three-two-two-one-two-one-five," Bishop replies steadily into the mic.

"Copy. Code confirmed. Standby, operator," the voice responds with a cool military cadence.

"Fuck yeah. We got 'em!" Bishop exclaims to Hawk before turning back to his communication device to relay more information. "We need rapid extraction, Overwatch. I repeat, this is Bravo-Charlie-Nine. Packet has been neutralized. Mission status is critical. Multiple casualties. We need an extract fucking pronto - " Bishop's voice is abruptly cut off by static.

"Negative on extract, operator. Midnight Sunrise Protocol has been initiated in your sector," the cold voice on the radio replies. "Eagles are approaching, thirty out. Over."

From Hawk' helmet cam POV, a half dozen townspeople carrying pipes, rifles, and large kitchen knives approach from a nearby alleyway. "Yo...we got company converging two buildings to the west. Status?"

"What the fuck…" Bishop gasps, turning back to Hawk before clicking his radio to respond, irritation creeping into his voice. "Assets are on the ground, I repeat, boots are still on the ground here, Overwatch. What the fuck do you mean - " The radio clicks three times and then - static.

"Status?!" Hawk barks at Bishop.

"What the fuck is Midnight Sunrise?" Bishop asks. Hearing those words, Hawk' face goes pale.

"We need to move. Now," Hawk says.

25

Deputy Cove's body cam offers a first-person view as he grabs AR-15 rifles, shotguns, and ammunition boxes from the metal lockers in the armory. He stuffs them into large canvas duffel bags on a rolling cart. A large wire cage encloses him in the room, with a few body armor kits and gun belts hanging from hooks on the cage. While it may not be an impressive armory by conventional standards - especially compared to what one might find in an inner-city precinct - the supplies seem more than sufficient for a small town, at least for a community accustomed to facing minor issues.

The heavy thud of combat boots on concrete echoes down the nearby hallway. Moments later, Hawk and Bishop burst into the room, breathless.

"We need to move now," Hawk barks, his tone catching Cove off guard. Without hesitation, Bishop strides into the room and grabs a duffel bag filled with weapons and ammo.

"Whoa. What happened up there? Did you get through? Is help coming?" Cove asks.

Before Bishop can respond, Connor enters alongside Hawk.

182

"Everything good back here? It's still quiet up front," Connor says nervously, glancing toward the main room where the damaged wall gapes open to the outside.

"No, it ain't," Bishop replies sternly.

"Listen up. We have less than thirty minutes to get out of town. We need the fastest transport you've got, and we need it now," Hawk commands.

"What do you mean thirty minutes? What's happening in - " Cove starts to ask, but Hawk cuts him off.

"They're nuking the fucking town. Us with it if we aren't gone. Let's move!" Bishop says, hefting the canvas bag over his shoulder and heading for the doorway.

"Nuke the town? You guys are messing with - " Connor begins, disbelief evident in his voice. Cove stands frozen in disbelief.

"He isn't fucking joking. Vehicles. What do you have?!" Hawk asks Cove in a tone that is all business.

"The impound. Benny Taylor's pickup... Farmer's kid, spoiled brat kept driving drunk, so we locked it up to teach him a lesson. It's in lockup out back."

01:49:25

At the rear of the building, the group moves quietly alongside the structure. Deputy Cove leads with a shotgun, while Connor, positioned in the middle, scans the area with his rifle, Das following closely behind. Hawk and Bishop jog at the rear, their automatic rifles trained on rooftops and surrounding sectors for any signs of threats.

"Right here," Cove says, pointing to a nearby garage. He pulls out a key ring and begins searching for the correct key to unlock the large sliding metallic door. As he fumbles with the keys, they slip from his grasp, producing a metallic tinkling that echoes off the surrounding buildings. Hawk and Bishop tense, scanning their respective zones for movement. Cove quickly retrieves the keys, hands shaking, and a small flashlight from his belt to see better.

"Hurry up! We've got movement to the right," Bishop hisses at Cove, signaling to Hawk.

Down the adjacent street, three disheveled townspeople shuffle along the sidewalk, their clothes tattered. An elderly woman drags a garden spade on the pavement, while another, clad in a butcher's apron, hefts a glistening meat mallet. In the shadows of the night, it's difficult to tell if the dark stains on the butcher's apron are fresh.

"My God... that's Barney Jiles," Cove murmurs. "The town butcher. I've known him since..." He trails off as Hawk hisses, "Ain't no time for reminiscing. He's gone. That ain't him anymore."

Cove returns to the lock and continues fumbling with the keys.

Das whimpers and starts to pull away from the group at the sight of the townspeople and their glowing blue eyes. "Hey! Stop! Stay close," Connor whispers.

Bishop reaches out and yanks Das by her arm, stopping her abruptly. She withers under his grip. "Stop or you're gonna die here," he warns, keeping his gaze fixed down the optic of his rifle.

Cove jangles the keys in the door and mutters curses under his breath. "God damn door, this old piece of shit always sticks..." He heaves his shoulder against the rusted corrugated aluminum door with a crash, and it loosens, sliding up a few feet as the metal groans. However, the noise draws the attention of the blue-eyed townspeople down the road. The butcher among them stops and focuses, his cold gaze locking on to Cove and his group.

"Shit. We've got contact," Hawk says. "Hold fire until they close in. We don't need any more attention. What's the holdup?!" he calls back to Cove.

"Help me lift this thing. It sticks, and it takes two people to budge it past here," Cove replies to Connor. Connor sets his rifle down and squats to assist Cove in deadlifting the heavy aluminum garage door. It creaks loudly, echoing through the back alley and into the street as it slides, gaining momentum until it slams to the end of the overhead track with a loud shudder and settles.

Inside the garage is a perfectly restored dark blue 1986 GMC High Sierra square-body truck, complete with massive off-road tires and KC lights. "Let's go!" Cove urges.

"Kid was spoiled... shit," Bishop remarks, clearly impressed with the truck.

Without wasting any time, Hawk and Bishop toss bags of rifles into the bed of the truck and usher the group inside the garage. Bishop helps Das into the center of the cab and buckles her in.

"I'll ride shotgun to cover you. Hawk, Connor, you two watch the rear and flanks and hang on tight. You're at the wheel, deputy. Don't obey the speed limit - we need to put the pedal to the metal all the way out of here if we're going to clear the blast radius. Copy?" Hawk commands.

"Can do," Cove replies as he climbs into the truck. Connor and Bishop scale the large tires and jump into the bed, closing the tailgate behind them.

01:55:54 09/23/22

From the perspective of the helmet cam and Cove's body cam in the driver's seat, we see the KC light bar flood the entire back alley behind the precinct as the engine rumbles to life.

"Is this thing gassed up?" Hawk asks. Cove checks the gauge and nods. "Good. Now step on it."

Cove revs the engine and floors it. The tires squeal as the pickup lunges out of the dusty impound garage and turns onto the nearby street.

The small group of townspeople are blinded by the truck's headlights, holding their hands with weapons clutched to shield their eyes. They stumble forward as the vehicle barrels toward them. Hawk leans out the window and opens fire, taking down the butcher and two other disheveled individuals in the truck's path. Cove doesn't swerve to avoid them; instead, he drives straight ahead, treating them like speed bumps. BUH-DUNK! The truck's lifted suspension barely notices the impact. Das screams and unbuckles herself, cowering down by the floorboards.

"Jesus, lady! Stay fucking put!" Hawk commands.

As they turn onto Main Street, the chaos and inferno of the town come into view. Smoke billows through the streets and buildings. Shattered glass litters the asphalt and sidewalks, the shards glinting in the flickering light.

BOOM! BOOM! From the bed of the truck, Connor fires his rifle behind them. Bishop follows suit with a burst of automatic fire.

"We've got company!" Hawk shouts to Cove. Cove slams the accelerator and weaves around wrecked cars, narrowly missing the bumper of a burnt-out sedan.

From Bishop's helmet cam, they see their pursuer behind them: a massive, shadowy hulk of muscle covered in black fur, with snarling fangs and piercing blue, fiery eyes. One of the wolves from the desert.

Connor fires multiple rounds at the lumbering beast, one shot hitting its mark and shattering the front leg just above the paw. The creature stumbles but doesn't falter completely. The wound that would debilitate any natural animal seems to be merely a minor inconvenience. The jagged bone of its front leg spurts blood as it stabs and splinters chips of bone with each rapid, plodding leap as it continues to chase after them.

Bishop empties his magazine into the animal with little effect before stripping the empty mag and slamming another into the lower receiver of his rifle, ready to reengage.

With each lunge, the wolf's true size becomes increasingly apparent through the video feeds. It is absolutely massive, standing four to five feet tall at the head and spanning at least six feet in length. The rippling muscles beneath its thick fur flex and tense with every leap as it closes the gap to the truck's rear bumper. The 4x4 weaves to avoid debris on the road and slows slightly as Cove struggles to maintain control at the wheel. Even at near full speed, this abomination somehow manages to keep pace with them. Now sensing an opportunity, the animal lunges, propelling itself through the air like a projectile of vicious claws, teeth, and murderous intent.

Bishop unleashes a volley of gunfire as the beast descends upon them. With jaws and fangs snapping just a few feet from landing in the truck bed - right on top of him, rescue flashes on screen in the most brilliant and unexpected form. A blinding flash and the rip of a plasma cannon blast send the wolf's body flying to the side. Moments later, a mesh of metal and muscle slams down on top of it. One of the enhanced cybernetic primates emerges, letting out a piercing howl as it stands triumphantly atop the crumpled form of the wolf. Although down, the wolf is not dead; it begins chomping and snapping at the cyborg primate. The two abominations instantly tangle in a grapple of teeth, fur, and bloody flesh illuminated by sporadic bursts of plasma energy.

The truck speeds on, leaving the embattled beasts behind. Through Connor's scope camera, flashes of the two mutants battling one another fill the screen. Wet chunks of flesh and fur fly through the air, backlit by bursts of bright purple plasma cannon fire before becoming shrouded in smoke from the smoldering town.

The main stretch of road leading out of Springerville and toward the highway is mostly empty, as seen through Hawk's helmet cam POV within the truck's cab. The last obstruction lies seventy-five yards dead ahead, where two sedans block the road - one flipped completely upside down and on fire. "Punch through! There's no time to go around," Hawk says.

"What if it kills the truck?!" Cove exclaims.

"We don't have time either way!" Hawk yells over the roar of the engine. Cove considers the thought for a moment and then slams down on the gas pedal. The truck roars to life, surging forward.

"Hold on!!!" Hawk shouts out the back window before bracing himself against the dashboard. The truck's steel bull bar crashes into the plastic frames of modern sedans, clipping their bumpers and sending them spinning off the road like tops in opposite directions. The truck jolts violently, but Cove quickly regains control of the wheel, pressing the gas once more.

02:05:17

From Hawk' body cam, the benign highway sign "THANKS FOR VISITING SPRINGERVILLE" glows ominously in the firelight, offering a macabre farewell as the truck speeds past.

"Approximately fifteen out! Everyone hold on!" Hawk yells back through the window, glancing at his tactical wristwatch. Cove has the gas pedal floored, and the truck races down the long, straight highway into the dark desert night.

02:12:35

The only sound is the full-throttle roar of the truck engine. Now on the outskirts of town, the burning skyline has faded to a flickering haze in the rearview mirror. From Deputy Cove's perspective behind the wheel, the distant silhouette of the mountain range comes into view, along with the imposing outline of the Dynamic Logistics installation carved into the rockface.

Unlike the inferno behind them, the Dynamic Logistics facility ahead appears still and untouched - no visible movement, no smoke, no outward signs of the horror they left earlier unfolding deep within what is now a high tech tomb. But everyone in the truck knows what lurks below the surface; they have seen enough to understand that something unthinkable has breached containment.

02:12:44 Dynamic Logistics Security Network – Internal Surveillance Archive

Multiple screens display surveillance footage from deep within the Dynamic Logistics installation, each window showcasing a different wing of the facility descending into chaos.

LAB 3A – BIOSYSTEMS DEVELOPMENT

A corridor bathed in emergency red lighting. Faint screams echo throughout. Two cyborg-enhanced chacma baboons charge down the hall, their blood-soaked cybernetic limbs pulverizing everything in their path. A scientist trips and screams, only to be torn apart before reaching the blast door. Security drones fire tasers ineffectively, soon dismantled by brute force. The feed jitters.

RESEARCH THEATER DELTA

A vast observation deck overlooks an enclosed arena where lab personnel scramble behind overturned desks. Autonomous attack drones hover into view and open fire. Muzzle flashes illuminate the pandemonium. Screams pierce the air as glass shatters and bodies collapse. A woman crawls toward an exit, but she is struck down by a burst of 5.56mm rounds, blood splattering the lens.

SUBLEVEL 7 – CONTAINMENT VAULT

A dark, grainy feed from deep underground shows alarms blaring and lights flickering. A technician frantically types commands into a workstation, attempting to initiate a lockdown. Behind them, a reinforced door begins to buckle inward under an unseen assault.

02:12:49
F-35 Lightning II – Targeting Feed – FLIR / HUD Overlay Active

The HUD glows steadily, with the targeting reticle fixed on the hardened structure embedded in the mountainside.

"Overlord, this is Valhalla Two-One. Target VORTEX is painted and primed. Requesting clearance to close the Iron Gate."

A pause follows, then static.

"Valhalla Two-One, Overlord copies. You are weapons free. Close the Iron Gate."

The pilot adjusts the throttle slightly, maintaining a steady arm on the HOTAS.

"Roger. Package hot. Two away."

From high above, two streaks of light slice through the night sky, rapidly descending toward the mountain.

The first bunker buster penetrates the upper blast doors of Dynamic Logistics. The second follows closely behind, punching deeper.

BOOM.

A massive fireball erupts from the mountainside, flaring from the reinforced entrance. Concrete, steel, and fire burst outward, captured in the slow-glow thermal feed.

02:12:52

Dynamic Logistics Security Network – Internal Surveillance Archive

A deep rumble shakes each individual feed simultaneously. The walls of every lab and sector ripple. Ceiling tiles tumble down. The few survivors shudder and stumble. Sirens wail and cut in and out. And then - fire. Brilliant flashes burst into each video pane, as balls of flame breach containment and consume the inhabitants in an instant. The cameras capture only fleeting moments of expanding flames and frames filled with terror. Then, one by one, the video panes cut to black - from left to right and top to bottom. Static. Dead silence.

02:13:01

AXON Body Camera: POV Deputy Cove – 4K, 60FPS

Inside the truck, the occupants brace themselves as a dust wave engulfs the highway, obliterating visibility. The truck shudders beneath them, its suspension bouncing as a thunderous rumble rolls across the desert floor.

"Fuck. Was that it?!" Cove yells over the sound of rattling metal, staring out at the massive fireball erupting from the mountainside.

"Negative!" Hawk barks back. "Preliminary strike! They just scrubbed the lab! That ain't shit compared to what's coming!"

Shifting his POV, Hawk looks through Cove's driver-side window, catching a faint glow from jet engines maneuvering the stealthy death machine above them.

26

F-35 Lightning II – Cockpit Combat Recorder – FLIR / HUD / MFD Active

The HUD and FLIR overlays flicker across the pilot's visor, with glowing green guidance and targeting symbology contrasting sharply against the desert landscape.

Far below, a pickup truck speeds down the highway, a streak of heat trailing from its engine block as it flees the burning town.

The pilot keys his comms.

"Overlord, this is Valhalla Two-One. I've got a vehicle egressing westbound, thermal shows four, possibly five pax onboard. Advise - do you want me to engage?"

A pause. Then the response, flat and clinical:

"Negative, Valhalla Two-One. Maintain focus on primary objective. Echo Grid Charlie is your target. Vehicle falls within predicted detonation radius and is considered non-essential."

"Copy. Holding target lock."

Another line from HQ. Colder still:

"Cleanup elements will sweep the outer boundary. Any outbound contacts will be resolved perimeter-side."

The pilot tracks the fleeing truck a moment longer through the HUD before shifting his gaze back to the town.

No further questions.

The F-35 roars overhead, slicing through the darkness - a wraith prepared to deliver unrelenting rapture on Springerville.

Ahead, the small town is already in the throes of self destruction at the hands of its once peaceful inhabitants and newly introduced residents from the lab. Flames consume the remaining rooftops, gas mains erupt like fiery geysers, and power lines writhe and crackle in the heat. Through the lens of the strike pod though, it's no longer a town; it's a hellish target grid.

The pilot steadies his hands on the controls.

"Valhalla Two-One to Overlord - objective in sight. The town is fully compromised. Confirm target zone."

Static, then:

"Overlord to Valhalla Two-One. Target confirmed. You are green. Midnight Sunrise is a go. Clean it up."

The pilot flicks a few switches in the cockpit. The screen blinks:

NUCLEAR ORDNANCE: B61 ARMED.
TARGET LOCKED.

The B61. One of the most tightly controlled assets in the nuclear arsenal. A precision-guided, low-yield tactical device - engineered for exactly this kind of operation: clean, compact, and plausibly deniable. Contained enough to pass, from a distance, as a large-scale industrial disaster. Designed not just to eliminate - but to vanish the truth along with it.

I've only seen footage of its use three times in the last ten years: Kandahar, Volgograd, and a classified site deep in the Congolese interior - erased from every satellite registry thereafter.

Each time, the result is the same. Absolute erasure.

The pilot exhales, calm.

"Package hot. One away."

From a belly-mounted ordnance camera, part of a classified avionics suite not included in any standard airframe diagram, the bomb becomes visible as it drops - a smooth, deliberate descent, tumbling end over end into the dark. As it falls, directional stabilizer thrusters engage in short, controlled bursts, fine-tuning its telemetry with mechanical precision. The F-35 banks hard, afterburners flaring, climbing away.

02:19:42 SPEC OPS Helmet Cams / AXON Body Camera: POV Deputy Cove - 4K, 60FPS /
AccuShot - Weapons Mounted HD Camera

From the ground, the night is deceptively quiet. The road hums beneath the truck's tires, the engine whining as it barrels down the open highway.

Then a brief flash - a pinprick of light over the desert horizon - and only for a mere second - stitching down through the clouds.

Hawk sees it.

"FUCK! Cover!" he shouts, wrenching the wheel from Cove.

The truck swerves violently, fishtailing as it leaves the asphalt and powers up an embankment. Gravel sprays as it struggles for traction on the desert sand. Then, the blackened sky behind them flashes with tremendous intensity… and begins to bloom.

02:19:45
F-35 Lightning II – Cockpit Combat Recorder – FLIR / HUD / MFD Active

From above, the screen whites out.

Detonation.

A blinding burst at ground zero - then a thunderous CRACK splits the air, a shockwave so deep, it seems to carry with it the wail of every soul hell has ever swallowed, rising momentarily into the living world.

A moment later, the shockwave washes over the landscape like a tidal wave. A wall of superheated dust sweeps across the desert floor, uprooting cacti, stripping brush to bare soil, and incinerating every living thing in its path.

The roiling fireball blooms outward, vaporizing concrete, steel, glass, and bone - devouring everything without pause or mercy.

SPEC OPS HELMET CAM - BISHOP

The ground-level view takes on an immense scale. The mushroom cloud metastasizing into the heavens, illuminated by the hellfire within, casting a reddish-orange glow through the haze. The wall of dust and ash curls overhead like an unscalable wall of mass destruction as it approaches the truck.

"Hold the fuck on!" Bishop yells, extending his legs and gripping the side of the truck bed. Connor's eyes widen in horror as he drops his rifle and curls up. "Hold on to someth - !" Bishop begins to yell again, but his voice is abruptly drowned out by the blast wave.

The truck is lifted off the ground, caught in the blast wind, tumbling like a toy car through the curtain of dust and light. In a split second, Connor's body is seen rag-dolling away before vanishing into the haze, his clothes tearing off. The camera distorts with static, and the final digital fragments of a few frames from Bishop's POV appear on screen as his body is propelled through the air. The fireball continues to ascend, its mushrooming column reaching into the stratosphere.

Back in the cockpit, the F-35 shakes in turbulence as the pilot escapes the blast zone.

His voice cuts in over the comms - flat, definitive.

"Valhalla Two-One. Sunrise complete. Target is gone."

ASSET RECOVERY

PART NINE

27

MIDNIGHT PATROL - RECON AND RECOVERY TEAM
RECONNAISSANCE DOCUMENTATION CAMERA - 4K

Midnight Patrol. The Custodians. The most meticulous cleanup crew the world has ever known. Strategically positioned, regionally designated response teams of highly skilled field officers on standby 24/7, deployed globally for this very purpose: to respond to the messiest of messes.

These specialists were specially trained and equipped to the highest standards to conduct operations on behalf of The Order. Their mission involved sweeping hot zones, retrieving significant artifacts, and thoroughly scrubbing sites that had, for all intents and purposes, already been scrubbed. They possessed tactical training and forensic certification, making them swift, precise, and studious in their work. Their recovery efforts were comprehensively documented on encrypted camcorders, allowing for review by analysts like me. This ensured that no detail was overlooked before archiving an event in the vault. If Dexter and John Rambo had their DNA spliced together in a lab and a small force of super sleuth soldiers were produced…well, that's how I'd best describe these stone-cold operatives: part forensic genius and part mission-driven psychopath who let nothing prevent them from completing their work.

Dressed in specialized, all-black CBRN protective suits and gas masks with self-contained electronic air circulation breathing apparatus, the Custodians arrived on site within thirty minutes of the event, surpassing even today's Uber Eats delivery standards. The video feed from the encrypted handheld camera captures the scene.

Nearby, a blacked-out, heavily fortified MRAP transport vehicle stands with a bright LED light bar. A surveillance spotlight mounted on the driver's side scans the horizon, its beam cutting through the haze. The fallout was undoubtedly in full effect, with radioactive particles contaminating every grain of desert dust in the area. Although the cap of the blast plume from the B61 had heavily dissipated due to strong desert winds, it still lingered high in the night sky, miles away. The thick, dark plume, backlit by firelight and moonlight, served as a fading fingerprint marking where the town of Springerville once stood.

The Custodian holding the camera trudges forward, heavy breaths filtering through the respirator mounted on their back, encased within their thick protective gear. These specially designed suits shield them from chemical, biological, radiological, and nuclear contaminants (CBRN). Subtle muffled chatter from the rest of the team can be heard on the communications channel as they navigate and survey the rocky terrain.

He advances as if on a Martian landscape, searching for evidence and artifacts. After a moment, a faint sound, almost imperceptible at first, breaks through the wind. Then silence. A moment later, it returns - a fragile, muted, and whimpering cry.

"Hel... Help. Help..." The vacant, desperate voice grows slightly louder as the Custodian moves through the dust-filled landscape. On the ground, splayed out with limbs outstretched, the barely recognizable form of Connor begins to come into view. His limbs are fractured and twisted in unnatural positions, his skin singed and blistered from the heat of the blast. The lone surviving hunter has fallen.

The Custodian approaches, and Connor gasps out his plea, fading fast. "Help. He-lp. Help... hel..."

The Custodian signals silently, and two others appear, and proceed to strip Connor of his backpack and scraps of clothing with medical shears. He is too weak to scream, but the grimace on his face says it all. Massive traumatic shock is likely the only thing shielding the dying man from what must be inconceivable suffering in his state. The Custodians aren't administering aid; that isn't their role when a civilian is so clearly beyond saving and the clock is ticking. They methodically begin to search him for artifacts.

One Custodian pulls Connor's cell phone from his blood-soaked pants pocket, while another rummages through his backpack and extracts a GoPro camera. Connor lets out a final "Help…" as his death rattle is distinctly heard, his eyes rolling back into his skull. The two Custodians pay no heed, simply bagging the items and sweeping the landscape with their flashlights, searching for more clues about these people and the "artifacts" they might possess. The Custodian team soon locates Connor's rifle with the thermal scope that recorded everything I've reviewed here shortly after this moment.

Then, slowly, from the POV of the lead Custodian's camcorder, the outline of the once-pristine, polished square body truck takes shape in the fog. Now crumpled and mangled, lying upturned on the driver's side, the prized collectible has been reduced to scrap.

The Custodian halts and tilts the camera down, revealing a severed arm lying at his feet, gruesomely torn just past the elbow joint. The only identifying markers are a tactical Garmin GPS wristwatch and a tattoo - Bishop. The rest of the body is missing as the Custodian moves around to the back of the truck, turning on his head-mounted flashlight to illuminate the entire truck bed.

He gestures toward the ground, and two more Custodians silently approach. In practiced unison, they unfurl thick black collection bags, scoop up the severed arm, and place it inside. One of them pulls a plastic drawstring, and the bag cinches shut with a quick ZIP! Tagged and bagged.

The camera shifts forward to the front of the truck. The windshield has been completely shattered, and the cab is partially caved in, obscuring the view inside. The Custodian bends down for a better look.

Slumped in the driver's seat is Deputy Cove, his body contorted and blood caked across his face from a large gash in his forehead, forming a mask of red. The whites of his lifeless, open eyes stare blankly at the ground. He's gone.

In the passenger seat, Hawk hangs limply, tethered by his seatbelt. The Custodian moves closer and shines his light on Hawk's face. As he reaches out, presumably to check for a pulse, Hawk coughs violently, sputtering blood. Tough son of a bitch - his survival instincts are kicking into overdrive.

The Custodian clicks the radio attached to the outside of his suit. Static blares loudly, then he keys it again and speaks.

"One survivor. Male. Thirties. Potential salvage," he states coldly, his voice muffled and monotone beneath the layered suit and respirator.

"Copy. Contain and transport for interrogation," a voice responds over the radio, sounding similar to the one from HQ heard previously through the headset comms of the fighter pilot. The Custodian stands and signals to his team. They rush to the crash scene, equipped with heavy extraction tools, a gurney, and medical bags. Moments later, one team member uses the mechanical jaws of life to free Hawk from the cab, while another administers an IV drip into his arm. The lead Custodian scans the thick air, able to see only fifteen to twenty feet into the desert beyond the wreckage.

The wind howls, and something nestled deeper into the recess of the truck cab, near the floorboard of the demolished truck captures his attention. The flashlight illuminates the dust, casting a soft beam into the compartment. A small hand, holding a blood spattered golden locket.

"Hold. We have one down here, by the floorboard. Goddamn miracle they weren't crushed...Status unknown," The Custodian says over the radio.

The Custodians maneuver in with extraction tools, crow bars, the jaws of life, and go to work dismantling the truck. Gradually, the body of Dr Anika Das is revealed. Within the collapsed cabin of the truck, she somehow managed to remain protected at the feet of Hawk and Cove. The Custodian waves a scanning instrument over her wrist and it beeps.

"HQ, mark that as two survivors: one male, one female. The female seems to be from the lab. Steady vitals, but banged up. We'll need med team support at basecamp to stabilize. All heat signatures from overwatch are now accounted for," the Custodian reports calmly as the rest of his team begins placing a neck collar on Das and brings in a stretcher board for transport

There's a crackle and static before a voice responds, "Bring her in. Priority. Scrub the scene." Then a burst of static punctuates the transmission.

"Roger," the Custodian confirms.

The sounds of sparks from welders and the jaws of life cutting through the truck cab drown out the chaos as they extricate Hawk and Das.

As soon as the survivors are extracted from the truck, a team of four custodians wearing incendiary packs and flame throwers steps forward. The scene erupts in an orange and yellow glow as streams of napalm belch from their hoses, engulfing the vehicle and incinerating all organic matter traces left at the crash site.

The feed cuts.

03:23:45
MIDNIGHT PATROL - RECON AND RECOVERY TEAM
RECONNAISSANCE DOCUMENTATION CAMERA - 4K

At the rear of the MRAP, the team of Custodians sits on two long adjacent bench seats, facing one another. Das lies strapped to a gurney in the middle row, eyes closed, IV bag and vitals monitors attached. No one speaks as the vehicle slowly comes to a stop and lurches into park. The rear double doors creak open, flooding the hold with bright white light.

The sound of the helicopter idling drowns out most other noises.

A blacked-out helicopter idles on the desert floor at the edge of the camp, with red flares flickering wildly against the rotor wash, marking an impromptu landing pad.

Beyond, a series of canvas tents connected by thick clear plastic corridors are illuminated by large portable emergency floodlights. The Custodians exit the MRAP, and the lead Custodian guides the team maneuvering Das on the gurney into the open air. Another MRAP offloads Hawk in the background. As the camera adjusts to the bright lighting, a massive decontamination and base camp comes into view. Clear plastic tents with decontamination showers are set up, while large, blacked-out transport freighter trucks park in a tight perimeter. Teams of Custodians move crates of gear between the trucks and the tented areas.

In the distance, a black suburban with dark-tinted windows comes to a stop. A Custodian approaches it, and as the rear passenger window rolls down halfway, a familiar face appears. It's Derringer, one of our facility directors - a senior man in his early sixties, with a craggy face etched by time, known for his fierce and exacting demeanor.

Derringer had been a Ref long before my time and had taken the mantle of higher responsibility in the last two decades, leading policy while remaining an active field operative when situations demanded it. It wasn't unusual for a director to arrive on site shortly after a major global event, but I was surprised to see him here for this situation. We had experimental labs worldwide producing some exceptionally advanced technologies. Yet this small town and experimental weapons lab had been thoroughly scrubbed. What could possibly have prompted him to make such a trip to the middle of po-dunk USA for what struck me as a virtually closed file at this point?

The Custodian approaches Derringer as he exits the suburban and produces a small handheld device resembling an IR thermometer. Derringer swiftly walks to Hawk on the gurney and scans his forehead with the small device. After a second, the machine beeps. Disinterested in the readout on the small screen, he moves to scan Das. The device beeps again and displays an unseen readout. Derringer, a notoriously expressionless Ref, studies the reading, and a flicker of curiosity briefly crosses his otherwise stoic face. Das's ID appears on the screen:

Personnel ID: Dr. Anika Das
   Age: 36
   Dynamic Logistics
   Clearance Level: Tier-4 / Genetics & Host Integration
   Nationality: Indian-American
   Specialty: Bioengineering & Neural Interface Design
   Status: Personnel Log Last Active – 21:43:12

Derringer points down to Das, nods to the Custodian, and Das' gurney is lifted into the helicopter.

As the helicopter's blades begin to spin, the Custodian steps back, his camera focused on the aircraft. One of the Custodians inside the chopper starts to close the door.

Das remains expressionless, staring blankly overhead. Dust swirls violently as the chopper rises off the desert floor, beginning to obscure the scene as the navigation lights pulse. Just before the sliding door fully closes, she turns her head slightly toward the Custodian - a faint flicker, almost imperceptible, in her eyes.

PAUSE. REWIND.

PLAY.

Flicker.

PAUSE.

REWIND - FRAME-BY-FRAME. ZOOM.

In the magnified frame, Das's face is frozen. The craft's lights strobe. Then…blue eyes. Just for two frames. A reflection of the aircraft lights? Ambient source lighting maybe? This is the kind of detail we Refs are trained to spot.

I open a window on the console screen and type a series of entries.

ASSET LOCATION: Dr. Anika Das > CASE FILE: SITE DD1525 > _100702_A_DD020
    ENTER

The cursor blinks for a moment, processing the request, then:

ASSET LOCATION CONFIRMED: Dr. Anika Das > CASE FILE: SITE DD1525 > _100702_A_DD020
    IN CUSTODY > MEMORY LANE > HOLDING CELL 213-B > INTERROGATION AND TESTING

Shit. They brought her…or it…here. To the hive.

FINAL TRANSMISSION

PART TEN

28

My mind races. We have one of the best anomaly holding cells on site, shielded and over-designed to contain every known and theoretical threat our engineers could dream up. This cell is reserved for the highest-priority cases. I deduced over the course of observation on this file that this particular anomaly was indeed a potential Class 5 case. A case: a consciousness, malevolent in nature, capable of commanding and controlling bodies like vehicles, whether living or recently deceased. Up to this point in the review, with the site thoroughly scrubbed, I had believed the case file to be resolved and was ready to make the official sign-off. But the Junior Arbiters had missed a cue. Flash frames. When a single frame in a video glitches, goes black, or shows an anomaly in one-twenty-fourth of a second, we call it a flash frame. As seasoned Arbiters, we can watch hours' or days' worth of footage, and we are expected not to miss a single frame of action that could behold a clue. Junior Arbiters are skilled but lack that depth of experience and that keen of an eye required. What some of us senior Refs may consider to be job security, I knew to be a potentially fatal flaw that could unwind the entire objective.

Beyond possessing organic matter, this entity demonstrated the ability to infiltrate advanced electronic interfaces to some unspecified but seemingly extensive degree. Dynamic Logistics had opened a door and let the devil in. Whatever form that came in. If that isn't cause for Class 5 concern, I don't know what is. My fingers fly across the keys, entering a flurry of access requests. I needed verification before initiating a lockdown order.

05:15:32 - 09/23/22 - CURRENT TIME
LIVE FEED ACCESS > AV > MEMORY LANE > HOLDING CELL 213-B > ENTER

A screen lights up, revealing the interior of a sterile cell. In the center, Dr. Das lies prone on an examination table, IV lines running from her forearms. A lab technician positions a mobile MRI machine above her head, while another technician stands nearby at a console, holding vials of drawn blood.

The room is quiet.

The technician operating the MRI flicks a few switches, and the computer console displays a readout of Dr. Das's skull and its internal structures. The camera feed from the security monitor flickers.

"Hey, take a look at this," the MRI technician says to his colleague, studying the screen.

The other technician approaches the MRI monitor and examines the image. He pinches the screen to zoom in, revealing a dark mass on the right side of Dr. Das's brain scan.

"What the hell is that?" the technician asks, moving closer to Dr. Das on the gurney. "Is that a USB?" He positions an overhead lamp above her head and brushes aside her matted, bloody hair. A small black USB port is embedded within a bloodied incision in her skull.

"What the fu - " the lab technician mutters as he retrieves a tray of surgical instruments nearby and leans in for a closer look.

My screen flickers.

Arbiters are trained in many capacities. We maintain composure in the most severe circumstances and face the most damning information while holding the line. We consider the fallout and devise outward-facing strategies to protect humanity from the harshest truths, all while upholding our nation's global objectives. We pride ourselves on maintaining an inhumanly low blood pressure. Mastering our physiology is part of the trade, allowing us to keep a hyper-naturally clinical and clear state of mind.

So when an Arbiter like myself feels the hairs on the back of their neck stand up, we know we are witnessing what we refer to as a "cataclysm" level event.

ZOOM

I control the security camera from my console, focusing on Dr. Das's face. Her eyes scan the room, tracking each lab technician as they examine her. Suddenly, she looks up into the corner of the room, locking her gaze directly on the security camera. My feed flickers again.

Understanding my role as an Arbiter is a double-edged sword. In the mind of a senior Ref like myself, there is little room for doubt, especially self-doubt. After decades of experience, we have seen it all. Despite having forged my pre-matter in a crucible of chaos and near-apocalyptic situations, when billions of years' worth of biological alarms ring through my consciousness, it either signals an impending crisis or the time to retire.

PING.

A window appears on my monitor.

LINGUISTICS DECRYPTION ANALYSIS COMPLETE.

ISS DATA INTERCEPT > DECYPHERED > 99.8% ACCURACY PROJECTED

My heart skips a beat as adrenaline surges. What many dismiss as mere coincidences in life, I have learned to dissect at a cellular level, revealing the intricate connections between seemingly implausible causes and effects. My finger hovers over the keyboard, my eyes darting between Dr. Das's intense gaze directed at the camera and the blank decryption window before me.

ENTER.

The screen goes blank, and the cursor flashes before a series of scrolling glyphs and symbols appear. This is the system's attempt to process the intercepted interstellar transmission and present it visually. These contents originate from the exact geolocation at the precise time of "the event" triggered by the Dynamic Logistics lab in Springerville.

The symbols, cryptic and glyphic, finish populating, and the cursor returns to the beginning of the string. As it advances, the system decodes and interprets them into plain English, achieving 99.8%

accuracy according to Arbiter systems standards.

"DOOM"
   "INSATIABLE."
   "LIFE."
   "FEEDS...ON...LIFE."
   "DOOM."
   "CONSUME."
   "SEED."
   "INFILTRATE."
   "DISSEMINATE."
   "DOMINATE."
   "DOOM."

Every cell in my body vibrates. The screen focused on Dr. Das glitches again, drawing my attention to her blue, glowing eyes.

The stated objective of the anomaly in plain English. Bridged by the rift at GD, this malevolent presence has declared its intent. And now... it has been brought, in the flesh of Dr Das, into Memory Lane - a Trojan horse.

29

Final Transmission

On the security camera feed, I watch as the lab techs back away from Dr. Das. She slowly sits up on the gurney, causing the techs to recoil in fear. As she reaches out to touch the MRI machine, sparks fly, and an explosion tears the apparatus apart.

The lab tech closest to the tray of surgical equipment scrambles to grab a syringe, presumably filled with sedative, but he isn't fast enough. Das flicks her hand, and the lights in the room explode overhead, showering sparks. Sirens blare as a dim emergency light activates within the lab.

Das rises to her feet, her glowing blue eyes scanning the room as she swiftly dispatches each lab tech, throwing one against the wall with a crash and grabbing another by the face, gouging her thumbs deep into their eye sockets. The screams are horrific, a symphony of terror and pain.

"Oh, fuck."

Floor-wide alarm bells begin to ring. Dr. Das exits the lab, and I tap a series of codes into my console to control access to the security cameras and follow her movements. She enters the main Hive hallway system and walks slowly down one of the main corridors leading to the center of the complex.

From another set of cameras, I see a team of security guard sentries rushing to engage her. With rifles ready, they round the corner and take aim at the doctor.

I don't expect the encounter to last more than a brief, violent moment. Our security division consists of top-tier war fighters. But Dr. Das - or whatever anomaly resides within her - possesses a capacity beyond my comprehension.

With a wave of her hand, the four-man team of sentries crumbles to the floor, their weapons scattering. Moments later, these men, sworn and trained to defend the hive at all costs, rise to their feet. Their eyes now glow with a sickening pale blue, transformed into drones serving another's will.

Now accompanied by her own security force, Das moves deeper into the hive. Waves of sentries attempt to intercept her, one after another, all meeting the same fate. Surrounded by a legion of guards, the once meek and seemingly helpless scientist has transformed into a Trojan war horse. She stops decisively before a bank of secured blast doors - the mainframe hall.

Inside the interconnected mainframe array room lies the heart, brain, and soul of the hive - our archives - but access requires a Master Level key card.

With klaxon alarms blaring throughout the hive, I toggle between security cameras.

I halt when I spot Derringer, bloodied and held at gunpoint, flanked by a group of possessed sentries. He possesses Master Level access, and now, so does Das.

All the pride I had taken in my training as an Arbiter - resisting extreme interrogation and torture, maintaining superior composure - diminishes as I witness Das effortlessly take control of Derringer's mind.

The stoic and formidable Arbiter's eyes now glow blue. He steps to the mainframe security door and inserts his override key card. The doors glide open, and Das strides through.

Alone in the massive cavernous mainframe space, Das proceeds forward. Gunfire erupts behind her, echoing through the halls of Memory Lane as possessed sentry guards clash with their unaffected comrades.

This is unprecedented, and my mind scrambles to comprehend the situation fully. Memory Lane has never been infiltrated, much less compromised, in all its years of operation. Admittedly, after reviewing this file, I realize we have never faced such a threat.

Das moves with purpose, scanning the room with her phosphorescent eyes until they land on an access terminal at the end of one of the seemingly endless rows of server racks. She glides to it and stops, reaching up to a small shelf filled with coils of cables. Retrieving a long USB cable, she inserts one end into the access terminal port and the other into the USB port embedded within her own cranium.

I can hardly believe what is happening. More automatic gunfire erupts from the hallway. The automated security system's voice blares over the loudspeakers throughout the building: *"SECURITY BREACH. MAINFRAME WING. INITIATE ENVIRONMENTAL CONTAINMENT."*

This is code for "gas the bastards." A few years ago, Memory Lane had a hybrid Halon system installed for fire emergencies. However, our unit is more than just a Halon fire-suppression system; it has multiple capabilities, including neurotoxic gas dispersion. The concept is that if our mainframe were ever physically attacked and a foreign or subversive agent was detected, we could neutralize the threat with a potent neurotoxin. While it wouldn't affect the equipment, any living entity would likely be reduced to a twitching mass.

From the ceiling, a thick, rolling gas surges from pressurized valves. The glowing mainframe racks, with their blinking LED lights, combined with the haze, create a disorienting light show.

I try to focus on the mainframe terminal screen in front of Das. The fog makes it difficult to see, but a series of glyphic symbols is rapidly scrolling across the screen - symbols identical to those from the ISS decryption. Das's head twists back at an unnatural angle as the gas envelops her, and the scrolling symbols flash in an increasingly rapid succession.

What is she doing? What is IT doing?

Then, Das collapses. Whatever infiltrated her mind may be otherworldly - perhaps from another dimension - but our meat chassis are still susceptible and mortal.

The answer to my question arrives sooner than I anticipated. On my computer screen appears an alert I never expected to see in my career or lifetime:

CATACLYSM EVENT. MASTER ARCHIVE DATA BREACH.

* * *

Those hairs on my neck are standing at attention again.

MASTER ARCHIVES > 100% FILE TRANSFER > GLOBAL DISTRIBUTION > ALLIES & ADVERSARY DISTRIBUTION LIST
   FULL DISCLOSURE.
   CATACLYSM PROTOCOL ENGAGED.
   05:23:59 CURRENT TIME

Timecode. My career depends on the accuracy of that time code. Everything we have ever discovered, documented, and catalogued occurred in fractions of seconds. These moments define the rise and fall of dynasties, determine the outcomes of mass casualty disasters, and influence the results of countless events - it all hinges on those brief intervals.

At five hours, twenty-three minutes, and fifty-nine seconds into this morning, time has stood still. For all intents and purposes, it ceases to matter. This is because I know what full disclosure really means.

The Master Archives has been breached and accessed by this malevolent entity. The impossible has become reality. It just unlocked every dirty deep state secret on record. Every volume of international espionage stored since the nation's foundation, every secret we squirreled away from past conquests and wars, countless undisclosed discoveries. The skeletons hidden in the bottomless pit of Memory Lane are now scaling the walls of the well and spilling out en masse to our adversaries. Undeniable admissions, war crimes, assassinations, and verifications of life beyond the stars that would shake every religious and societal pillar to rubble...are now in the wind.

In this scenario, once merely hypothetical, the inevitable outcome has always been the same: global annihilation, cataclysm, doom.

Our advanced AI has run countless simulations to determine possible outcomes, and each has ended the same way: global thermonuclear war. It might begin as expected - riots, rebellions, confirmed accusations leading to impossible reparations between nations, which escalate into full scale ground wars. Some scenarios even suggest that the U.S. would attempt to frame the leak as disinformation, a hack, or a cyberattack to undermine our country. Yet, the unbearable weight of undeniable truth always crushes public faith.

Here we stand: a malevolent force unleashed by our own government in the pursuit of technological superiority has opened a door that cannot be closed. We have released a force with a clear objective: to doom our civilization, spread chaos, and ultimately eradicate us by utilizing the one thing that can destroy us more effectively than brute violence: it has held up a mirror. It has revealed our darkest truths and exposed our best-kept secrets, fully aware of how we would react.

I take a deep breath. Processing the sheer volume of data being released to our adversaries will likely take at least an hour. First, there will be twenty minutes of shock and awe, followed by internal discussions about the reasoning behind such a disclosure. Some might even entertain the possibility that it is a massive hoax intended to mislead. However, this speculation is irrelevant; revealing just one or two data points to China, Russia, North Korea, or Iran could be enough to spark a war. For each of these adversary nations, we have numerous assassination plots on file, past, present, and future conspiring, any of which could prompt them to launch warheads into the stratosphere.

Cataclysm. 05:23:59 - 09/23/22.

The most important moment of my life - and of all humanity, really. In under an hour, there won't be anyone left to report to. No record to document anything at all…that is my assessment.

No record at all. At least not here on Earth.

The thought stirs something within me. It will require every bit of training, every ounce of resolve and focus to encapsulate what I have witnessed in the short time we have left.

I open my reporting window, fingers poised above the keys. I have less than an hour to report on the last and most consequential event that has ever occurred in human history. This story. How it all came undone.

My magnum opus.

BEGIN ARBITER AFTER ACTION REPORT > UPLOAD TO ISS > SATELLITE ARRAY ARCHIVE > DEEP SPACE TRANSMIT > REPEAT SIGNAL
AFTER ACTION REPORT TITLE: CATACLYSM
* * *

More From Redacted Press

Thank you for reading CATACLYSM.

To learn more about upcoming releases, visit:
www.theredactedpress.com

About The Author

About the Author

Scott Conditt is an author and filmmaker based in Arizona, where he lives with his wife and three children. He writes science fiction and tactical thrillers that combine technical authenticity with cinematic storytelling.

In addition to his fiction, Scott is a journalist and writer in the tactical, defense, and firearms industries, and a writer/director/producer whose commercial work emphasizes character-driven stories and visual intensity.

* * *

www.ingramcontent.com/pod-product-compliance
Lightning Source LLC
Chambersburg PA
CBHW032115020726
47494CB00007BA/2079